The Sins of the Father

The Chronicles of Detective Marcus Rose

(Volume 3)

By

A.D. White

A.D. White

www.adwhite.net

<u>Acknowledgements</u>

Thanks to my wonderful family and friends who have supported me and encouraged me to follow my dreams.

All characters are the work of the author's imagination. This book is a work of fiction and not meant to depict real life events.

**Cover Illustration by
D.J. Jackson, HF Productions**

A.D. White

CHAPTERS

Page

1. Hold On — 9
2. Four Weeks Ago — 13
3. One Layer at a Time — 21
4. Can I Say it Now — 25
5. Daddy Issues — 31
6. Bass Reeves — 39
7. That Bitch Set Me Up — 49
8. Father Time — 61
9. No Words — 67
10. Close the Door Behind You — 73
11. Stephanie Ross — 79
12. Naomi Reed — 81
13. Sarah Murphy — 83
14. Verbal Dyslexia — 85
15. Abrams Armored Carriers — 89
16. Samuel Abrams — 97
17. Sebastian Eckert — 99
18. Purpose and a Little Patience — 103
19. Cabin in the Woods — 119
20. My Brother's Keeper — 129

Chapter One
Hold On

Logan slammed on the brakes and the tires squealed as his vehicle slid to a stop in front of the emergency room at Charles Regional Medical Center. The ER staff was on standby and quickly pulled Marcus out of the back seat and onto a stretcher. As they rushed him down the hall, Marcus' vision began to dim. He stared up at the ceiling as each fluorescent light fixture raced by. The ER doctors and nurses were talking a mile a minute as they evaluated and treated Marcus. To some it might have looked and sounded chaotic, but in reality it was a symphony of medical science and exactly what he needed.

"BP 82 over palp and falling", "tachypnea at 30." "Take his vest off", "we have diminished breath sounds on the right side, think we're looking at a pneumothorax." "Get me a chest film, AP and lateral. Massive bleeding from his left thigh, the bullet must have hit the femoral artery." "Clamp it and let's hurry up and get him to surgery. He's going into shock, time is not on his side, Go, Go, Go."

Marcus could hear what they were saying in the background, but felt his consciousness slipping away. Periods of his life flashed through his mind like an old black and white picture show on a giant screen. He saw himself playing with his siblings in the backyard of his childhood home...playing football for the local boys club...His high school graduation...Scenes of basic training in the Air Force...His wedding to Gina...His sons being born...Walking across the stage at his police academy graduation... As if to say a life well done!

Marcus clinched his fists and sighed in an attempt to hold onto life. He wasn't ready to die, but how many people really are? There was so much more that he wanted to accomplish. So many things he hadn't seen. Things that he had done and wished he could change. Was it too late? Is this how I'm going to die he thought to himself before he started reciting the Lords' Prayer in his mind? Our Father who art in heaven... The last thing he heard was Logan saying "hold on man, please hold on!" Then he saw his father reaching out to him as he slowly lost consciousness.

Gina hurried into the emergency room escorted by two uniformed police officers. She was frantic and crying. She saw Logan and rushed to him asking "what happened Logan, what happened?" Logan looked clouded in confusion as he searched for words to explain how they got to this point. "We were arresting this maniac when he pulled out a gun and shot Marcus." Just then, Dr. Crystal Allen walked over and asked "are you Mrs. Rose?" "Yes," Gina replied, "how's my husband?"

"He's in critical condition right now and in surgery. He was shot three times and has two major injuries" explained Dr. Allen. Gina and Logan looked at her in anticipation as she continued. "He was shot twice in the chest but thank God he was wearing a vest. Even so, the force of the bullet broke a rib on his right side which punctured his right lung causing it to collapse. We put in a chest tube and that's being addressed in surgery. The major issue is the gunshot wound to his left thigh. It pierced his femoral artery causing massive bleeding."

Logan tried to provide support to Gina as her body seemed to go limp while the doctor continued. "The femoral artery is the main artery that provides oxygenated blood to the tissues of the leg. It passes through the deep tissues of the thigh region of the leg parallel to the femur. It's also the second largest artery in the body. This is problematic because damage to that artery has caused him to lose a massive amount of blood, which in itself could kill him. Also, if he survives this, he could lose the leg due to insufficient blood flow throughout that leg. We won't know anything until he gets out of surgery and then it's a wait and see game at that point."

By this time the Chief of Police and other top officials in the police department joined them and heard the diagnosis from the doctor. They tried to offer words of encouragement to Gina. Saying things like "he's a strong man", "he's a fighter", "he won't give up." Gina didn't really hear much of what they said. All she saw were lips moving as she wondered how she would tell their two boys what happened to their father. Was history repeating itself? She looked at Logan once more and emotionally asked "what happened?" Logan replied "well, it all started four weeks ago."

Chapter Two
Four Weeks Ago

It was Saturday night in Washington, D.C. with a cool spring breeze blowing in the air. Marcus was out to dinner with his favorite lady, his wife Gina. They had just ordered their meal. Marcus playfully informed her "think carefully about what you order. The higher the price, the higher my expectations will be for tonight." "Really, I think I will order this fifty dollar steak. What's that tell you" Gina asked with a seductive smile? Marcus continued "what it tells me Mrs. Rose is that your dress will be coming off as soon as we get through the front door." Gina smiled "well, I guess I'm gonna have to pay up. Wouldn't want to break any of your man rules." Marcus stared into her eyes with a devilish grin and began to ask "do you have on any..." when Marcus' work phone rang. His whole demeanor changed as he reluctantly answered the phone. "Detective Rose," oh really, okay," he nodded his head. "Fort Lincoln? Yeah, I know it. Copy that" he said, putting his phone back in his pocket. Gina raised her hand and got the waiters attention. "We're ready to order and we'll need this to go" then looking at Marcus anticipating the bad news that their date was ending prematurely once again.

"Sorry babe. Homicide over in Northeast. I'll drop you off at home." Gina was all too familiar with being the wife of a homicide detective and all the complexities that came with it. But at times like this, familiarity didn't make it any easier. "We need a vacation Marcus. For once I'd like to have one night out that isn't interrupted by death," said Gina with a hint of frustration. "You're right babe. I'll put in for some vacation time next month. Anywhere you wanna go" replied Marcus. "You owe me Marcus" she said playfully. "You can't just threaten me with a good time and run off to work." "Oh, my word is bond Boo. When I get home tonight," as he shook his head "you better watch out." "Promises, promises detective. You just be safe out there" Gina said as she stared into his eyes. Marcus dropped Gina at home and watched her walk to their front door. After all this time, he still enjoyed looking at her from behind. He took a deep breath, and then proceeded to his assignment.

Marcus arrived on the scene of a middle class neighborhood in the Fort Lincoln section of D.C. It was a pleasant neighborhood. Nice townhouses, single family homes, well-kept front lawns and unusually quiet streets. A slice of heaven in a city that was known for its violence. "Looks like the gangs all here," he thought to himself as he saw several marked police cars, the crime scene investigators and the medical examiner vans outside of the residence. Marcus removed his trusty miniature hand sanitizer bottle from his jacket pocket, squirted some on his hands and vigorously rubbed them together. As he approached the front door, he flashed his badge to the officer who was securing the scene.

"I know who you are detective," said Officer Davis. "I helped you with one of your cases last year." "Oh yeah, I remember" said Marcus. Will, right?" "Yes sir," he replied. "You still studying for the investigator's test" Marcus asked? "Yep, gonna pass it this time." Marcus smiled "speak it into existence and it'll happen" as he handed the officer one of his business cards. "Let me know if you need any help" Marcus said as he started to enter the residence. When Marcus took his first step, he felt glass under his shoe and immediately looked down. He looked up at the porch light and noticed that the bulb had been broken. "Watch out for that glass" he told the officer. "I'm gonna have crime scene photograph and collect that" then he entered the residence.

His partner, Detective Logan Steele, was already on scene. "Detective Rose" he playfully joked. "Thanks for dropping by. Did you pick me up coffee on your way here" he asked? "Yeah, you a funny guy Logan" as Marcus put on a pair of rubber gloves. "Remind me to laugh later". Marcus was tired and a little grumpy which was unlike him. He usually enjoyed verbally sparring with Logan. Truth be told, it was the best part of their work days. The two were like brothers. But even brothers get on each other's nerves at times.

"What do we have here Detective Steele" Marcus asked? Logan shook his head and began "we have a white female, twenty five years old, both hands cuffed to the headboard, laying face down on the bed. Fully clothed in a pair of pajamas. She has a stab wound that entered from her back and exited out of her chest. No murder weapon found but the blade has to be at least twelve inches long. Nothing looks out of place. No signs of a sexual assault, but the M.E. (Medical Examiner) will give us a definite on that. Plenty of valuables are still here. Television, laptop, jewelry and cash in her purse. No signs of forced entry. The place was locked shut when a unit arrived a few hours ago to check on her." "Check on her? Why" asked Marcus? The dispatcher got a call from an unknown male reporting that there was a dead woman inside." "Really" Marcus replied with a puzzled look on his face. "Yep, the number was blocked, but the call is recorded." "You say all the doors and windows were locked" Marcus asked? "Yep, one of the responding units pried open the living room window and entered that way. I looked for her house keys but didn't find any. It appears that the killer was safety conscious and locked the door behind him." "Not funny Logan" Marcus barked. Logan barked back "Damn man, what's up your ass today?"

"I'm sorry Logan, just got some crap on my mind. I'm good man, but you still ain't funny" he said with a smile. "What's the vic's name?" Logan looked at his notebook "Sarah Lee." Marcus chuckled "really? Like the lady that makes pies? Stop playing man." "No bullshit Marcus, her last name is Lee. Nah, I'm kidding. Her last name is Murphy." Marcus just shook his head and let him have his playful moment realizing that his attempt at humor was a coping mechanism. Cops often used humor or sarcasm to deflect the seriousness of the moment. Marcus and Logan then entered the master bedroom to examine the body. Marcus thinking to himself out loud "the knife seems to have entered the region of the back directly in line with the heart. Massive blood lost."

Logan interrupted "Marcus. You wanna hear something stupid?" "No" replied Marcus. Logan continued "well, I was trying to get the twenty dollars that Smitty owes me. He's whining about not having the money and then he says "as long as I owe you, you'll never be broke." Logan threw his hands up in the air "what kind of shit is that? Him owing me doesn't put money in my pocket. I'm still broke. That's the dumbest saying that I've ever heard." Marcus chuckled "that's just like when someone says he wants his cake and eat it too. As if that's a bad thing. What else am I gonna do with the cake?" They both laughed. "Okay, focus man and help me examine this body. You see that rash around her nose and lips" Marcus asked. "Yeah, what is that" Logan replied. "Don't know yet. Hopefully the M.E. can tell us."

Another squad detective arrived on scene. *Detective Katelyn Alverez. A sexy, no nonsense Latina who was meticulous at her job. Long black hair worn in a ponytail with an hour glass figure. She's been in homicide for four years. She goes by the nick name Al. She was the oldest of four girls and her father is a retired*

D.C. cop. She and Logan tried to date last year but it didn't work out. She was very fond of Logan and respected him as a colleague but has trust issues. Seeing that Logan does have monogamy issues, her mistrust was actually well deserved.

"Hello ladies" she greeted Marcus and Logan. "What do we have here?" Logan stepped up and said "I'll handle this" as he pulled out his notebook. "The vic is Sarah Murphy. Handcuffed to the bed and stabbed through the back with a very long blade. House locked up with no signs of forced entry. Nothing missing that we know of." Al looked at Marcus and said "wow, your puppy's well trained." Marcus was a little surprised by that statement. I guess he wasn't the only one in a bad mood tonight. "You guys need to work it out." This is exactly why you don't date your co-workers, Marcus thought to himself as he started to leave the room. "Oh, did anyone else notice that the front porchlight was broken, with half the bulb still in the socket" Marcus asked? Logan and Al both shook their heads no. "Have crime scene photograph and collect it as evidence" Marcus directed.

The last member of the squad was Detective Frank Callahan. *Detective Callahan was tall, slim and clean shaven. He had been in homicide for a year and a half, very intelligent with a Master's degree. Liked to demonstrate his extensive knowledge of the dictionary, considered himself a Wordsmith. He looked like a younger version of the professor in Gilligan's Island.*

Thus they nicknamed him "The Professor". "I overheard that sparkling dissertation from Detective Steele and as always, his facetious attempt at humor. What do you need me to do Marcus?" "Let's spread out and check the rest of the house. Look for anything out of place or curious looking" said Marcus.

The detectives checked the entire house before re-assembling in the living room. "Find anything interesting" Marcus asked the group? Al spoke up "found the number 347 written on the bottom right corner of the mirror in the first floor bathroom in what appears to be blood. I'm assuming it's the victim's blood. I'll have crime scene photograph and test it." "Okay thanks" said Marcus. "Let's all do a canvass of the neighborhood. Make special note of any cameras the neighbors might have in their front or back yards. It would be nice to have this person on film." I'll release the body to the M.E., and will see everybody at roll call tomorrow morning.

Chapter Three
One Layer at a Time

Roll call began at 0600 hours. It was their new sergeant's first day with the homicide unit. His name was Reginald Powell. Detective Steele worked with him many years ago while assigned to the Eighth Police District. Sergeant Powell was a hard worker and paid attention to detail. A great guy, but he had his own idiosyncrasies which meant that he would probably fit in perfectly with this group. He liked to give words of wisdom to his subordinates but half the time no one knew what the hell he was talking about. Every now and then he would mumble, which really confused the troops.

For that reason, he earned the nickname "Mumbles." The officers didn't say it to his face, but referred to him as Sergeant Mumbles. Lieutenant O'Malley and Sergeant Powell entered the roll call room. The lieutenant started off by saying "I'd like for everyone to meet Sergeant Reggie Powell. Now that Sergeant Gant has retired, Sergeant Powell will be the squad sergeant. I expect that you will give him the same respect that you gave Sergeant Gant." The lieutenant then gave a nod to the sergeant.

"Good Morning everyone. As the lieutenant said, I'm Sergeant Powell and it's a pleasure to be working with such a distinguished group of detectives. Your reputation precedes you. I've been on the department for twenty years and did my last stint in the Warrant Squad. I'm gonna sit back and let you guys (indistinct mumbling) until I know my way around the homicide cases. I go by the mantra "If it ain't broke, don't fix it". Logan leaned over and whispered to Marcus "and thus is why they call him mumbles." Marcus smiled but wasn't going to let Logan make him lose his composure in front of the new sergeant. Of course, that's exactly what Logan wanted. He would like nothing more than for Marcus to laugh out loud and piss off the new sergeant on his first day. But that wasn't going to happen today.

Sergeant Powell turned his attention to roll call. "Detective Rose." "Here Sarge" responded Marcus. "Detective Steele." "Present Sarge" said Logan. "Detective Alverez." "Aqui" responded Al as she always did. "And last but not least Detective Callahan." "Here Sarge" said Callahan. "And let me also add that it's a pleasure to work with you sir." Logan looked at Callahan and said "you just gonna kiss up to him right in front of us, huh?" All the detectives laughed, including the lieutenant.

"All right, settle down" joked the sergeant. "Let's go over Saturday night's case assigned to Detective Rose." Most detectives would refer to their notebooks while briefing on a case, but not Marcus. He had the information in his notebook but also committed every detail to memory. "The victim's name is Sarah Murphy. She was found handcuffed to her bed and stabbed in the back and through her heart. She lives alone, according to neighbors, and didn't seem to have many visitors. Nothing appeared to be taken or disturbed. All the doors and windows were locked but the victim's keys were missing."

"Her mother lives out in P.G. County and was notified of her death. She's coming in this morning so we can find out all we can about her daughter. Oh, and crime scene did their usual, printing and photographing. However, we found a couple of peculiar things." "Go on" said the lieutenant. "The bulb to the front porch light was broken, but left in the socket and the number 347 was written in, what I assume was the victim's blood on the bottom right corner of the first floor bathroom."

Sergeant Powell seemed intrigued "I think that Fairfax County might have had a similar case with the victim stabbed and handcuffed. Call over to their homicide unit and see if there are any similarities between the two cases." "Copy Sarge" said Marcus. "Do we have a preliminary time of death yet Marcus" asked the lieutenant? The M.E. puts the time of death around two a.m. Saturday morning."

"Did we get anything from the canvass" asked the sergeant? Detective Callahan chimed in "the neighbor two doors down has a camera mounted on the side of his house that faces his front door. It also captures part of the side walk of the house adjacent to the victim's house. About eleven p.m. the previous night, it captured an ominous figure dressed in black walking in the direction of the victim's house." "Ominous, huh" remarked the Sergeant. "Threatening, menacing" said Callahan. "I know what it means" responded Sergeant Powell "and I like your choice of words detective." Callahan smiled and nodded.

"Okay, good work" said the sergeant in a pleasing tone. "Detective's Rose and Steele don't limit that call to just Fairfax County. Call all the neighboring jurisdictions and see if they have any similar cases. My Spidey senses are tingling on this one." They both nodded in acknowledgement. "Alverez, interview the mother when she gets here and Callahan check with the M.E. and see if you can expedite the autopsy." They all acknowledged their assignments. "Okay, fall out" directed the sergeant. "And remember" he added "You can only peel an onion one layer at a time!" Logan looked at Marcus and grinned "words of wisdom brought to you by Sergeant Mumbles."

Chapter Four
Can I Say It Now

Jennifer Murphy, the mother of the victim arrived at the detective's office to be interviewed. Al greeted her "good morning ma'am. I'm Detective Alverez and I'm so sorry for your loss" as she reached out to shake her hand. Al walked her to one of the interview rooms and asked her to have a seat. "I'd like to know everything that I can about your daughter in an effort to help find who did this. First, do you know of anyone that might have done this?" Ms. Murphy started to cry "I don't detective. I've been racking my brains trying to make sense of this, but I just can't," she responded.

"Was your daughter seeing anyone" Al asked? "No, not that I know of. Her last relationship ended over a year ago." "Could he have done this" Al inquired? "I don't think so. There was no animosity between them, but I guess that anything is possible. "Is her father in her life" asked Al? "No, her father and I never married. He was in her life up until two years ago. He mysteriously stopped coming by and stopped calling her. He just disappeared and no one knows what happened to him. It's like he dropped off the face of the earth" she replied. "Did she work or go to school" ask Al? "She worked at the District Federal Credit Union on H Street, in

Northeast and was attending night school at UDC (University of the District of Columbia)."

"Has your daughter ever been arrested or involved in drugs ma'am" Al asked? "What's that got to do with her being murdered" Mrs. Murphy asked with a puzzled look on her face? Al moved closer to her and placed her right hand over the hand of Mrs. Murphy "I'm not sure that this has anything to do with her murder ma'am, but every little detail that we find out about your daughter may lead us to a clue. Sometimes the littlest detail can help us find a killer."

"Okay" said Mrs. Murphy. "My daughter was a good person but not perfect. There was a time in her life that she experimented with drugs and led a promiscuous lifestyle. But a few years ago, she cleaned herself up and went back to school. "What type of drugs did she take and where did she get it," asked Al? Her mother sighed "marijuana and cocaine, but I have no idea where she bought it. I only know about her past lifestyle because we had a heart to heart talk after her father disappeared. She was a daddy's girl and took it hard. He too had his struggles before he turned his life around."

"Thank you so much Ms. Murphy. Can you write down her ex boyfriend's name and phone number for me and if you think of anything at all, please give me a call. Also, write down her father's name too" as she handed her a business card. "I will detective and you can expect a call from me every few days to find out if you've found the animal who killed my daughter" displaying her ire. "I'll definitely keep you in the loop, Al assured Mrs. Murphy. Also, does the number 347 have any meaning to you" as they both stood up. She thought for a few seconds and replied "no, why do you ask?" "Just curious" responded Al as she walked her out of the office.

As Marcus and Logan were calling surrounding jurisdictions, Detective Callahan returned from the medical examiner's office and briefed them. "As we thought, the stab wound was the cause of death. There were no signs at all of a sexual assault but the M.E. found something ostrobogulous on the body." Marcus perked up. "The substance around her mouth and nose was chloroform." "Chloroform" Marcus remarked. "I thought they only used that on television and in books." "Real life can be stranger than fiction" said Callahan.

Marcus turned around to his laptop and quickly googled chloroform. "Used as an anesthetic in 1847. First tested on animals and then used in dental surgery. It has a sweet smell and high doses may result in death. It takes about five minutes to render someone unconscious and was discontinued because it caused deaths due to respiratory failure and cardiac arrhythmias. Wow, you learn something new every day" remarked Marcus. "That you do" as Callahan nodded in agreement.

Sergeant Powell walked over to Marcus and asked for an update. Marcus briefed him on the findings of the medical examiner as Logan walked over to join them. "I don't know if this is good news or bad news, but Prince William County, Virginia has a case very similar to ours" said Logan. "A few months ago, they had a murder of a black female, thirty years old, found handcuffed to a chair in the dining room of her townhouse. She was stabbed in the back and through the heart also." Everyone's eyes lit up. "Did you ask them if any writings were found on the mirror" asked Marcus. "Of course I did and the answer is yes. They found the number 205 written in blood on the bottom right hand corner of the mirror in the first floor bathroom. And before you ask, the front porch light bulb had been broken out also."

"Good work Logan" commented Sergeant Powell. "Keep calling around while I brief the lieutenant." "This is big and I'm almost afraid to use the term that I'm thinking of." Logan looked at Marcus and began to form the words when Marcus interrupted "don't say it." Logan said "Okay, but just cause I don't say it doesn't mean it's not true." "Just because they're similar doesn't mean that they were committed by the same person" said Marcus. "We gotta be absolutely sure before we open that can of worms. Let's keep calling around and see if any other cases are similar."

About an hour later, Detective Callahan walked over to Marcus' desk with a painful look on his face. "Montgomery County has a case just like ours. White female handcuffed to the bed, a single stab wound through the back and the number 347 written on the bathroom mirror in blood." "Wow" said Marcus. "I guess it's true." Logan looked at him and asked "can I say it now?" "You might as well" Marcus reluctantly replied. "Serial killer. We have a serial killer in the DMV (D.C., Maryland and Virginia)."

A.D. White

Chapter Five
Daddy Issues

Logan noticed that Marcus had been a little pre-occupied for a few weeks. He hadn't been his normal even keeled, cool, sarcastic self. "Let's take a ride Detective Rose" he suggested to Marcus. Marcus tossed him the keys "Okay, but you're driving." They both got into the car and Logan went through his normal pre-driving ritual. Slowly adjusting both side view mirrors and then the rear view mirror. He starts the car, and then adjusts the driver's seat to give him enough leg room. He turns on the radio. All the while, Marcus is just staring at him with that look on his face. The look that sarcastically asks could you do this any slower? "You drive like my grandmother" barked Marcus. "Has your grandmother been in any accidents" asked Logan. "No" said Marcus. "Exactly" replied Logan. "I'll drive and you just sit over there and enjoy the ride. I know what I'm doing" as he finds the right radio station. I've been driving since I was six" he joked.

"Let it Be" by the Beetles was playing. "You don't know nuthin about this, do you Marcus" joked Logan? Marcus considered himself a student of music and knew some of all genres. "Young man, I'm well familiar with this song. You're gonna need to dig a little deeper to stump me" said Marcus. Logan began to sing along with the song. Off key, I might add. "When I find myself in times of trouble, mother Mary comes to me, speaking words of wisdom, Let me be. Let me be, let me be, let me be, oh let me be. Speaking words of wisdom let me be." Marcus just stared at him in amazement. "That ain't the words" Marcus said with laughable disgust. "The name of the song is "Let It Be," not "Let me be." Logan put the car in reverse, looked over at Marcus and said "you sing it your way, and I'll sing it the right way." Then he backed the car out of the parking space and continued singing "Let me be, let me be, let me be, oh let me be. Singing words of wisdom let me be."

Marcus put his left hand on his forehead, closed his eyes and said "God, please help me. For this fool knows not what he does." Logan smiled "now that you're finished praying, let's talk." "Okay, what's on your mind" asked Marcus. "You my brother" replied Logan. "You've been different lately, everything cool at home" Logan inquired? Marcus sighed deeply "yeah, everything's good at home, I've just been thinking about my dad lately. Today is the anniversary of his death." "Wow, I'm sorry man. I had no idea" replied Logan. "He died on the job, right" asked Logan?

"Yeah man. My pops was a great dude. Always there for us. Loving and strong. I always looked up to him. Wanted to be just like him." "Damn, I wish I had the chance to meet him" said Logan. "I've heard old timers make comments about him but wasn't really sure what to believe" said Logan. "Don't listen to the gossip,

I'll tell you the truth about my old man. I heard all the rumors about how he was a dirty cop so I dug deep into it. I talked to cops who worked directly with him. I've read the classified reports of the event that lead to his death. He was a damn good detective and went undercover with the Vice unit. He was in deep cover for about a year, never reporting to work at his unit. He became entrenched into his cover of being a middle man between a drug cartel and a major D.C. drug dealer. Street cops that he knew would see him, but he couldn't acknowledge them or he might blow his cover. After a while, some just assumed that he was dirty but in actuality, he was on the job."

"Wow" said Logan, "tell me more." He gave the department all the information of when a major shipment was due to be delivered and even revealed the top guy was going to be there. The S.W.A.T. team moved in and there was a shootout. My father was caught in the cross fire and was shot in the head. They were never really sure if he was shot by the drug dealers or the cops. He was a hero, but some chose to sully his name without having all the facts.

People gossip and pass on bogus information from person to person. After a while, the story changes and people treat lies as fact when they really have no idea what the truth is. That's one reason why I hate gossip. He's the reason that I'm so meticulous about everything I do on the job. I leave no room for speculation. There's very little grey with me. Black and white brother, everything's black and white. Everything has its place and everybody's got their lane. As a detective, I've got things that I'm supposed to do. Things that are my responsibility. The sergeant and lieutenant have their responsibilities. I don't try to do their job and they don't try to do mine. I know my lane and I'm not concerned about things I have no control over. Gina says that I'm predictable but I'd like to think of it as methodical. Having everything in place calms me. It gives me comfort. It's the unknown that keeps me up at night."

"Wow, that's deep" said Logan as he shook his head. "I'm speechless." Marcus smiled "that's a first." They both laughed. "You know that you're like a big brother to me? You're one of the few men that I look up to. My parents divorced when I was young and my father wasn't around much after that. When I needed advice on women I had to look to the streets for the answer. I need your opinion on something." "I got you Logan. You know that I will always give it to you straight" said Marcus. "Yeah, I know. That's why I'm gonna share this with you. But first, is this a no judgment zone?" Marcus laughed "this is not Planet Fitness but no, I'm not going to judge you (this time)" he mumbled under his breath.

Marcus was intrigued. He always enjoyed listening to Logan's female drama. "What's on your mind Grass Hopper?" Logan sighed deeply "it seems like wherever I go; I seem to leave a trail of angry women." Marcus chuckled lightly. "Don't laugh man, I'm serious. I'm not sure what I'm doing wrong. For example, I went to lunch last week and happened to run into an old friend of mine. I have fond memories of her, but apparently she didn't share that sentiment. I walked over to her to say hello. She looked at me with such hate and disgust in her eyes and said "if it isn't Logan Steele." "She said that she had been thinking about me lately, which I thought was a good thing. Like a dummy, I said that I'd been thinking about her too. She laughed and said part of me will always love you Logan, but part of me will always hate you too. I don't want to sit here and make small talk with you. Do me a favor and just go away. And just like the song says "if you see me on the street, walk on by. Just walk on by." She had the nerve to start singing the damn song." Logan went on to say "it shocked me. I'm really not sure why she was hurt. We had a good time. She knows what type of guy I am. I never told her that we were exclusive. Never said I loved her. So you tell me Marcus, what did I do wrong?"

"Whew, where do I start" Marcus sarcastically said with a smile on his face. "Some women want more than just a good time." "What else is there" Logan asked with a perplexed look on his face. "How about trust, security and someone that actually cares for them" Marcus answered. "I don't wanna do the love thang man" as he shook his head. "Scared, huh" said Marcus. "I ain't never scared; I just don't wanna look like a fool." "It's painfully obvious what the real problem is" said Marcus. Logan just stared at him, waiting for his response. "You don't want to be vulnerable. If I didn't know any better, I'd think that you've been hurt before and now you're reluctant to care about anyone, because it will make you vulnerable. And because of that you want what you want, when you want it and you keep them at an arm's length. Relationships don't work that way. It's about give and take. Taking chances and being willing to compromise." Logan just looked at Marcus with a stupid look on his face. You know, that look when you know that the other person really just doesn't get it or doesn't want to get it.

Marcus continued "sometimes there can be strength in vulnerability. Your problem is that you really don't play well with others. It's not about you all the time. You know that I love you like a brother, but you lack empathy and compassion when it comes to women. They're just play things to you instead of being real people with real feelings. I know that what I'm about to say is a strange concept to you, but take a breather. Leave the women alone for a little while. Just do you!" "And how could that possibly help," asked Logan. "I don't know man. If you sat back and just observed things, it might give you a different perspective.

"The old Logan Steele sleeps with a woman a few times and then ghosts them. You stop answering their calls and you don't have time for them anymore. You disappear from their lives. How are they supposed to feel about that?" Logan started to answer but was interrupted by Marcus "No, don't answer that. It was a rhetorical question. You showed them their worth and then you make them feel worthless. You're too old for that man. At what point in your life do you want substance over indiscriminate sex? Put yourself in their place. Is this how you want to be treated?" Logan looked at him and said "I know, it's a rhetorical question." Marcus grinned "yep, sure is. A lot of people can't understand the other person's plight unless they walk in their shoes. They can't fathom why someone feels the way that they do, because they don't have a place of reference."

Logan spoke "I never lie to them. I never tell them that I love them or ever promise them a future." "Maybe you didn't lie to them with words, but your actions lied. They say one thing today and another thing tomorrow. In the beginning you treat them like you love them and make them think that there's a future in store. How would you feel if someone did that to your mother, or your sister? How about if you ever have a daughter? Empathy my brother...empathy."

Logan sat in silence for a few minutes taking it all in. "I wish that I had a man to tell me that a long time ago. I missed out not having my father to guide me through the complexities of women." Marcus laughed "look at you using big boy words. Looks like we've both got daddy issues."

A.D. White

Chapter Six
Bass Reeves

Now that the team has come to the realization that there's a serial killer walking the streets of the DMV, notifying the press was the responsible thing to do. The public had the right to know. They still weren't sure of the connection between the victims and who could be next.

The lieutenant prepared a press release and sent it to the department's Public Information Office (PIO). The press release didn't give any intimate details of the crime. Didn't mention that the numbers 205 and 347 had been written in blood on the mirrors. It did state that the victims had been bound and stabbed, but didn't offer the fact that they were handcuffed or the location of the stab wound. You never want to give out too much information for fear that another sick person might want to duplicate the murders. Without that intimate knowledge, if someone did attempt to duplicate them, there would be distinct differences in the crime scenes.

Figuring out the pattern of the killings was the next best way to identify the man behind the crimes. How did he pick his victims? What did the victims have in common? Was it random? What was the meaning of the number 347 or 205? Marcus rarely believed in coincidences. Everything had a meaning. One thing was for sure, there is a connection, but finding that connection wouldn't prove easy.

There's a reason that serial killers do what they do. It's not by happenstance. Something in their life drives them to kill. Sometimes it's a traumatic event that unleashed the crazy inside their head. Sometimes it's DNA. All these questions had to be answered if the detectives were going to solve this case.

Now the research began. It was time to find out everything they could about the victims and their routines. Trace their daily steps. In doing so, determine if the paths of the three victims have ever crossed. What did they have in common? Marcus was tasked with tracing the steps of the first victim that lived in Virginia, Stephanie Ross. Logan was responsible for tracing the steps of the second victim who lived in Maryland, Naomi Reed. Al was responsible for tracing the steps of the third victim who lived in D.C., Sarah Murphy. Detective Callahan assisted all three with their assignments by continuing to search for other cases similar to theirs and creating a dossier on each victim.

Years ago, Marcus had attended the FBI National Academy at Quantico, Virginia. He was nominated by his agency head to take a professional course of study due to his demonstrated leadership qualities. One of Marcus' favorite courses there was in behavioral science which featured serial killers. This was his first serial killer case and the knowledge he gained there could be essential to solving this case.

At roll call, Sergeant Powell asked Marcus to brief the squad on his knowledge of serial killers. Marcus was the primary on this case but every member of the squad had specific responsibilities and was essential to solving this case. If they were going to be successful, it had to be truly a team effort.

Marcus stood, "serial killers are a special kind of criminal. They are manipulative, aggressive and impulsive. They have no specific type of upbringing. Some were abused or neglected as children; however the list of serial killers with normal childhoods is pretty long too. For example, Ted Bundy and Jeffrey Dahmer. Those guys both grew up in what were considered normal households.

Serial killers, even as children, seek control over the lives of others. At a young age they kill small animals because it's the only type of creature they will be able to fully dominate. They don't show any regret or remorse when caught doing something wrong. They have no feelings at all about what they've done. They're cunning and smart. Since they know right from wrong, eventually they learn how to mimic empathy, which helps them fit into society.

Some may seem weird or distant, but others seem perfectly normal. Many have families and homes, are gainfully employed, and appear to be normal members of the community. In other words, they hide in plain sight and appear to be just like everybody else. But that's an act, an imitation. And contrary to popular belief, serial killers come in all different races." Logan interrupted "say it ain't so."

That lightened the moment and everybody laughed. Marcus continued "I'm sure you all remember the D.C. Sniper. He was black." Logan interrupted once more "damn, damn, damn" as he shook his head. "Most serial killers are men" Marcus continued. "In the last hundred years only fifteen percent of serial killers in the U.S. were women. So even though it's possible it's a female, we're probably looking for a man."

"Why do they kill?" "Can they help themselves" asked Al? "Each one has their own personal motives. There is no single identifiable cause or factor that leads to the development of a serial killer. It's complicated. Just like everybody else, it's a combination of heredity, upbringing and the choices they make. Sometimes a single traumatic event can trigger their actions. But make no mistake about it, they choose to do what they're doing."

Detective Callahan interjects "so due to the façade they have created, it indubitably could be anyone." Marcus answered "yeah, basically, but there is good news." Everyone waited with baited breath. "They possess certain personality traits that can be exploited, particularly their inherent narcissism, selfishness, and vanity. Couple that with the fact that the longer they kill without being caught, they may become lackadaisical and take shortcuts. They already feel like they're smarter than everyone else, especially the police. So they start taking short cuts and become careless and that's when we get the upper hand. Sometimes they test our resolve and intelligence by leaving clues for us to find and figure out. It helps them feel superior. Sooner or later even the smartest criminal makes a mistake. I believe that's why this killer left those numbers on the mirror. He threw us a bone because he believes we're not smart enough to catch him without his help."

It took a few days, but the team did their best to trace the victim's steps for the last thirty days of their lives. Where did they go? Who did they see? Where did they work? What restaurants did they visit? Did they exercise? What gyms did they attend? Did they attend church and if so, where? Every detail they could think of had to be addressed. Maybe they could find that common thread that linked the victims.

They first noted all the similarities that linked each case. All the victims had been stabbed from back to front and through the heart. Each victim had traces of chloroform around their lips indicating that the killer may have used it to incapacitate them. Each victim had been handcuffed to either their bed or a chair. The number 205 or 347 had been written in the victim's blood on a bathroom mirror. And finally, the front porch light of two of the victim's home had been broken. These facts unquestionably linked all the victims to one killer.

After that, they asked probing questions and each detective would provide the answer aloud. Marcus asked "what are the dates of each homicide?" Logan answered "the first one occurred on February 2nd. The second one on April 2nd and the third one on July 2nd." "Okay, each one happened on the second day of the month. The number two has some type of meaning. I don't believe in coincidences."

Marcus asked "did anyone else have their car serviced at the One Stop Auto on Richmond Highway?" "Nope, not mine" answered Al. "Not mine either" answered Logan. Marcus asked "did any of them have their alarms monitored by Fast Response Alarms?" Al sat up straight in her chair. "Yes, Sarah Murphy used that company and her alarm was not set the morning of her murder." "Stephanie Ross' alarm was not set either" said Marcus. "Naomi Reed lived in an apartment and did not have an alarm system" added Logan.

"This is the first connection that we've found with any of the victims" said Marcus. "We need to find out if Naomi Reed was ever approached by Fast Response.

Who solicited the other two and who actually installed their alarms" asked Marcus? The possibility of a connection put a twinkle in Marcus' eyes. "Logan and I are headed to their local office right now to find out the answer to these questions." Marcus tossed the car keys to Logan "let's go, I ain't got all day detective." "Are you sure that you can stand more of my driving and singing" joked Logan? "Yeah, you right. Give me those keys back. I'll drive and you just put your seat belt on and be quiet. For real though, I wouldn't exactly call that singing. Sounded like you were in pain to me." "Real funny Marcus, the women love my singing" said Logan as he looked over at Al. Al rolled her eyes "you sound like a wounded dog, howling at the moon." "Let's go Marcus. All this praise is making me sentimental" Logan sarcastically remarked.

They hurried to the car and put on their seat belts. After starting the car, Marcus pulled out his travel sized bottle of hand sanitizer and cleaned his hands. Logan looked over and said "you know, you should probably clean your hands after using the steering wheel, rather than before." Marcus looked back at him with a smirk on his face, but said nothing. Then put the car in gear and drove off.

During the drive to the alarm company, Logan asked Marcus a very profound question "If you could have dinner with any person, dead or alive, who would it be?" Marcus laughed and answered "Jesus Christ."

Logan looked at him with contempt "besides Jesus Christ, who would it be?" "My father" Marcus replied. Logan began to get a little frustrated, which was exactly what Marcus intended, even though his answers were honest. "Okay, last time smart ass. Besides Jesus Christ and your father, who would it be?"

Marcus quickly responded "Bass Reeves." "Who the hell is Bass Reeves" asked Logan. "You call yourself the police and you don't know who Bass Reeves is" asked Marcus? "No I don't. Educate me" responded Logan. "Alright, sit back and learn something youngin. Bass Reeves is the person that many believe was the inspiration for the fictional character The Lone Ranger." Logan scoffed "really?" "Yes really. He was the first black U.S. Marshall West of the Mississippi. He was credited with arresting over 3000 felons. He shot and killed 14 outlaws in self-defense. Was born into slavery in 1838 and served in the American Civil War. Later, he fled north into Indian Territory where he lived with the Cherokee, Seminole and Creek Indians and learned to speak their languages until slavery was abolished by the 13th Amendment. He was then recruited as a U.S. Deputy Marshall in 1875 because he knew the Indian territories and spoke several Indian languages. He served 32 years as a federal peace officer. He had eleven children and once had to arrest one of his sons for murder. He died in 1910."

Logan was astounded that he had never heard that story and even more astounded that Marcus did.

"How do you know shit like that" he asked in amazement? Marcus laughed "man, I've got a ton of useless information stored up here" as he pointed to his head. "Is that why your head is so big" Logan said as he laughed aloud. "You really amuse yourself, don't you" said Marcus as he chuckled at Logan's comment. "You gotta know your history Logan. It's important to know where it all started." Marcus' answer was just as profound as Logan's question and once again, Logan was impressed with Marcus' intelligence. It was part of the reason that he looked up to him. Even though he would never admit it, he strived to be like Marcus.

A.D. White

Chapter Seven
That Bitch Set Me Up

Marcus and Logan arrived at Fast Response Alarm and walked up to the front desk. Sitting there was a very pretty receptionist. She looked to be in her mid-twenties, dark skinned with long jet black hair and a smile that lit up the room. Just as Marcus was about to introduce himself, Logan stepped in front of him and said "Good Morning Beautiful." She smiled and replied "good morning, how can I help you?" Logan pulled out his credentials and showed her "I'm Detective Logan Steele and this is my driver, I mean my partner Detective Rose." Marcus was unamused by his greeting. Classic Logan Steele, so he let him take the lead. "We need some information on who might have serviced these three addresses (as he showed her the addresses from his notebook).

"Let me check the system and see. Can I ask what this is in reference to?" "Just a slight problem with how the system has been operating." "Oh, okay" she replied with a confused look. After a few minutes she said "the same employee installed the Virginia and D.C. address, but I don't show that we have a system at the Maryland address. Marcus and Logan looked at each other like they just hit the jackpot. "What's the employees name and how can we reach him" Marcus asked? "Well, his name is James Poole and he should be coming in shortly. "Here's his picture" as she rotated her screen so that they could see.

"Great" said Marcus. "I'm curious; do your people have employee numbers?" "Yes they do" she replied. "His employee number wouldn't happen to be 347 or 205, would it?" "Let me check. No, it's 1482. All our employee numbers have four digits." Marcus scoffed with disappointment. It was a long shot, but he had to ask. "Thank you ma'am, you've been very helpful" said Marcus. "I didn't get your name" commented Logan. "It's Angela. Angela Lewis" she replied.

How tall are you she asked? "6'5" replied Logan. "I like tall men" she said with a smile. "I like women who like tall men" Logan countered, which generated an even bigger smile from her. Logan handed her his business card "I really appreciate your helpfulness today. I feel like I should repay you in some way" he said with a devilish grin. "That won't be necessary" interjected Marcus. Logan turned and looked at Marcus with contempt. "As I was saying before my driver so rudely interrupted. Since you helped me, I feel that I should repay you in some way." He noticed that she wasn't wearing a wedding ring. "Do you think that your boyfriend would mind if I took you to lunch?" She laughed "I don't have a boyfriend at the moment." Logan smiled once again "I'm so sorry to hear that. So lunch is a possibility?" "Yes detective, lunch is a possibility." "Great" Logan replied. "My cell number is on the card; let me know when you're free."

Marcus and Logan went to the parking lot and decided to wait for Mr. James Poole. This was a solid lead and they didn't want to waste any time following it up. After a few minutes, a black pickup truck pulled into the parking lot and a tall skinny gentleman got out. "Looks like our guy to me" commented Marcus. "Yep, that's him" Logan agreed. They quickly got out of their vehicle and stopped him as he was about to enter the building.

"Excuse me, are you James Poole" asked Marcus. "Who wants to know" was his reply? Logan flashed his badge "the police want to know." "Okay, what's this about" Mr. Poole asked, then said "no matter what that bitch says, I didn't do it." "This is going to be good" Marcus thought to himself. "What bitch might that be" asked Logan? Realizing that he just put his foot into his mouth, Mr. Poole decided to just shut up and didn't respond. Marcus wanted to defuse the situation before it became adversarial. "We have some questions about a couple of places that you installed alarms. The occupants are into some shady business and you might have seen something inside of their homes that can help us solve a crime." "Why didn't you just say that in the first place" he replied as he gave Logan a mean look. Logan sneered back as he thought to himself "don't make me beat dat ass."

"Can you meet us down at police headquarters" Marcus asked. "On Indiana Avenue" he inquired. "Yes, so you are familiar with the place" said Logan? He gave Logan another mean look, but did not answer. "Let me notify my supervisor and I can meet you there in hour." "Let the guard at the front desk know that you're there to see Detective Rose and someone will walk you up to our office. We really appreciate your help Mr. Poole" said Marcus. "Anything for the police" he said with a tone of sarcasm.

James Poole arrived early and was escorted to the Detective's Bureau. Marcus greeted him and shook his hand "thanks for coming Mr. Poole. We really appreciate it." "You're welcome detective" he responded. "Your partner's not going to be in on the interview, is he?" "Yes, he will be in the interview" responded Marcus. A look of disappointment flashed across Mr. Poole's face. "Why do you ask" inquired Marcus? "Your partner has..." Mr. Poole paused as he searched for the right words. "Your partner has an attitude that I don't care for and find disrespectful." As Mr. Poole was finishing his sentence, Logan walked up from behind him and stood next to him and glared in his direction.

"The interview room is this way" Logan said as he pointed in the direction of the room. They all went into the interview room as Sergeant Powell and Lieutenant O'Malley watched from the observation deck. Detective

Alverez was running Mr. Poole through the NCIC (National Crime Information Center) data base to see if he had a criminal record. Marcus squirted some hand sanitizer into his hand and rubbed them together vigorously before he began.

Marcus: First of all, let me re-introduce myself. I'm Detective Marcus Rose and this is my partner Detective Logan Steele.

Mr. Poole: (acknowledged by nodding)

Marcus: We wanted to talk to you today because there might have been criminal activity in some of the homes that you serviced. It's possible that while you were installing the alarm systems, you might have seen something that could help us out.

Mr. Poole: What type of criminal activity?

Marcus: Well, I'm not at liberty to disclose that information right now. You know, it's an ongoing case. The things that we're going to ask you about happened a while ago. How's your memory in general?

Mr. Poole: I have an excellent memory detective. I have a mind like a steel trap (as he smiled with pride).

Logan looked at Marcus as to ask "what the hell does that mean?" Marcus just grinned because he knew exactly what Logan was thinking.

Logan opened a folder and pulled out a paper with Stephanie Ross' address in Virginia, Sarah Murphy's address in D.C. and Naomi Reed's address in Maryland. He placed it on the table in front Mr. Poole as he sat.

Logan: These are the addresses that we're curious about.   And also, I just want to let you know that this interview is being recorded on video (as he pointed to the camera in the corner ceiling of the room)

Mr. Poole: (Beginning to feel a little uneasy) I'm here to help you, right?

Logan: That's right; you're here to help us. (As he nodded in agreement)

Mr. Poole: (Picked up the paper and looked at the addresses) I installed the systems in the D.C. and Virginia addresses. I've never been to the Maryland address.

Marcus: You do have a good memory. Okay, can you tell me about the install at the D.C. address first?

Mr. Poole: What do you want to know?

Marcus: Just tell me what you did and what you saw. Any tiny detail might help us.

Mr. Poole: You know, I went in and talked to, Sarah I think her name was. Told her that I was going to put sensors on all the downstairs doors and windows. Set up her control box and showed her how to work it. Set up her alarm code.

Marcus: Did you notice anything in particular about the inside of the home?

Mr. Poole: No, not really. It was neat and clean and she wasn't bad looking.

Logan: You said that you set up her alarm code. Do you remember what her code was?

Mr. Poole: They tell me what code they want to use, but I don't record that information anywhere.

Logan: Do you remember what code she chose?

Mr. Poole: Ah, no. No I don't.

Logan: You told us earlier that you had an excellent memory. You know...the steel trap thing. Was that a lie?

Mr. Poole: No, it wasn't a lie. It would be unethical for me to memorize or record that type of information.

Logan: I'm sure that you wouldn't do anything unethical, huh? Would you remember the layout of the homes? You know the floor plan. Keep in mind that you have a self-proclaimed excellent memory.

Mr. Poole: What is this really about? Do I need a lawyer?

Marcus: (Marcus took on a serious tone) Did you do anything wrong?

Mr. Poole: No, of course not!

Marcus: Then why would you need a lawyer?

Mr. Poole: I don't!

Marcus: Okay, you remember Sarah Murphy. What about the home in Virginia?

Mr. Poole: Stephanie Ross, I think.

Logan: Wow, you remembered her name. Why?

Mr. Poole: No particular reason. I told you that I have a good memory.

Logan: No, you said that you have an excellent memory. I have a good memory. I remember shit like, she had a nice body, her house was messy, but I'm terrible with names. You installed her alarm system a year ago and you still remember her name. I've slept with women and don't remember their names, but enough about me!

Mr. Poole: What are you saying detective?

Marcus: Have you been back to either home since installing their alarms?

Mr. Poole: No and I don't like the implication that I've done something wrong. Are you asking me this because of what that bitch said?

Marcus and Logan glared at him without answering.

Mr. Poole: Look, my old girlfriend is a liar. I never broke into her house, never put my hands on her and never threatened to stab her. That bitch set me up!

Marcus and Logan looked at each other and tried to contain their surprise. Just then, Detective Alverez entered the room and gave Marcus the results of Mr. Poole's record check. Marcus looked it over, and then handed it to Logan.

Marcus: (Leaned closer to Mr. Poole) Understand this Ronald. When I ask you a question, I already know the answer. I'm really trying to determine whether you're a liar or a truthful person. My detective's intuition tells me that you just may be a liar.

Logan: (Moved in closer and shuttered at what he smelled) Why did Ms. Pamela Scott apply for and receive a Stay Away Order on you? Says here that you're not allowed to come within a thousand feet of her, her job or her home address? What in the world could you have done to elicit that type of response from her?

Mr. Poole: (Stood up quickly and yelled) I know my fifth dominion rights.

Logan: (He tried his best not to laugh, but couldn't contain it) Do you? I don't even know your fifth dominion rights but I do know your Fifth Amendment rights. Sit your ass down while I read them to you.

Mr. Poole: (Remained standing)

Logan: (Stood up) I said, sit your skinny ass down before I (Marcus gave him a look that said "don't say it".)

Mr. Poole: (Sat down) I don't like where this is going.

Logan: Well, you're gonna love this. You have the right to remain silent. You are not required to say anything to us at any time or to answer any questions. Anything you say can be used against you in court. You have the right to talk to a lawyer for advice before we question you and to have him with you during questioning. If you cannot afford a lawyer, one will be provided for you. Do you understand these rights?

Mr. Poole: Yes and I want a lawyer! I want one right now (as he slammed his hand on the table).

Marcus: Doesn't work that way pal. We're going to end this line of questioning. You're free to go and contact a lawyer on your own. Let us know who's representing you and we'll contact your lawyer the next time we question you. And we will be talking to you again.

Logan: Wow, you seem kinda violent. You may have an anger problem Mr. Poole. I'd suggest that you seek counseling for your anger issues.

Mr. Poole: You are one sarcastic bastard detective.

Logan: My level of sarcasm depends on your level of stupidity Jamie!

Mr. Poole: That's James detective. James!

Logan: Okay Jamie (he said with a smile).

Marcus: (Stood Up) You're free to leave. Let me show you the way.

Marcus walked Mr. Poole to the elevator and made sure that he left. He walked back into the office where he was met by the Lieutenant O'Malley, Sergeant Powell and the other detectives. "Was it me or did his breathe smell like he just ate a shit sandwich" joked

Logan. "Nah, it wasn't you. He could have used a tic-tac or two" said Marcus. "A tic-tac or two? He needed that hold damn container" Logan laughed. "Good job men. Let's contact his ex-girlfriend and get the story on this clown" said Sergeant Powell. "Do we like him for this" asked Lieutenant O'Malley? "A strong possibility" said Marcus. "His ass did it" commented Logan. "Detective Callahan, complete a comprehensive background check on this guy" said Sergeant Powell. "Al, I want you to interview his ex."

"I want to know everything possible about this guy before we question him again. We should know the last time he took a shit" said Lieutenant O'Malley. "That's a bit much L.T." Logan said sarcastically. "Professor, you take care of that" Logan joked. All the detectives looked at Logan like "shut the hell up." Sergeant Powell barked "Okay, we don't have all day people. Let's go to work. We got a (indistinct mumbling). They all went to their desks. Logan looked at Marcus as if to ask what the sergeant just said. Marcus hunched his shoulders "I don't know what he said. I don't speak mumble!"

Chapter Eight
Father Time

In the middle of Roll Call the next morning, Lt. O'Malley walked in with the morning newspaper and slammed it down on the desk. "Look at this crap" he blurted out with disgust. "The headline to the Metro section stated "Serial Killer Evades Police" and they even refer to him as the Boogey Man because he sneaks in and out at night without being detected. They're giving him just the publicity that he wants. Glorifying him. I'll bet he's sitting back with a cup of coffee reading the morning paper as we speak." Marcus interjected "he's feeling himself now as narcissists do. He thinks he's smarter than us and in the end that will work to our favor." "How so" asked Sergeant Powell?

"He's getting comfortable, reading his own press. And when people get comfortable they make mistakes. And sooner or later he'll make one too. That is, if he hasn't already. It's up to us to find that mistake though, and we will" said Marcus with the confidence that his peers admired about him. His confidence was contagious as it inspired the other squad members to be confident. The entire squad felt confident that they could solve this case.

"All our asses are on the line if we don't catch this bastard. I had a meeting with the Commander of Homicide and the Chief of Police yesterday and, as you can imagine, they are extremely interested in this case as is the whole DMV. They don't want any excuses. If we don't catch this guy, I'll be walking a foot beat on the Potomac River. And I won't be by myself" as he glared at each detective in the squad. We need to catch this guy ASAP," shouted the Lieutenant!

"I'm on it Lieu. On my way to interview Mr. Poole's ex-girlfriend now" said Al. "Okay Alverez, work your magic. We need a break" said the Lieutenant. Detective Alverez drove to Pamela Scott's apartment in the DuPont Circle neighborhood of D.C. As she knocked on the front door, she noticed a camera on the top corner of the house pointing in the direction of the front door. Although it's not all that uncommon, she took note of it. Al rang the doorbell and immediately heard "how can I help you?" "My name is Detective Alverez from the D.C. Police ma'am. I'm looking for Pamela Scott." "I'm Pamela Scott. How can I help you?"

"Do you know a man named James Poole?" There was a pause, then "I know him and his ass ain't supposed to be nowhere around me." Alverez smiled "he's not ma'am, I just want to ask you some questions about him." "What did he do now" she asked? "Can we talk about this inside ma'am" replied Alverez? A few seconds later she heard the sound of three locks being released. The front door opened and a short, chubby woman stood there with a disgusted look on her face. "Can I see your credentials" she asked. Alverez removed her wallet containing her badge and I.D. from the inside pocket of her jacket and flipped it open for her to see. "Okay. You can never be too careful these days" she said with measured relief, then unlocked the screen door to let Alverez in.

After Alverez entered, Pamela Scott peered outside, scanning from left to right. She then re-locked the screen door before closing and locking all three locks of her front door. Alverez took a mental note of this also and wondered why she looked so paranoid. As they sat at the dining room table, Alverez asked how she knew Mr. James Poole. "I'm ashamed to say that I used to date him." "Ashamed? Why" asked Alverez?" Ms. Scott explained that James Poole was a very smooth operator. "He knew just what to say and just what to do to win your confidence. And as soon as you slept with him, the abuse would begin."

"First it was mental abuse. Being controlling and intimidating. And if you didn't do exactly what he wanted, the abuse turned physical. He went from being Mr. Charming to Mr. Scary." She also explained that he had a fascination with knives. He always carried a knife with him and would threaten to cut her heart out. This went on for a year before Ms. Scott summoned the courage to apply for a stay away order, which was granted. She hadn't seen Mr. Poole since, but always had the feeling that she was being watched. Since he installed security alarms for a living, she was sure that he could defeat any alarm and gain entry to her house. Thus explained the camera and multiple locks at the front door. The back of the house was just as fortified. Pamela Scott asked "what did he do?" "We think he might have hurt someone" replied Alverez. "A woman" she further inquired. Alverez nodded yes. "I knew it. He's capable of anything" she said with conviction. "Do you think he's capable of killing someone" Alverez asked? With a concerned look on her face, she nodded yes. Alverez left there convinced that James Poole was their man, but it was still obvious to her that this case lacked a motive. There's always a reason why people kill. Doesn't have to be a good reason, but a motive was imperative to any case.

Alverez couldn't wait to get back to the office and brief the squad on her findings. She figured that they could set up twenty-four hour surveillance on Mr. Poole and catch him in the act. Case closed! As she drove back to the Homicide Division the dispatcher came over the radio with a look out for a black male, approximately 18 years of age, slim build, five feet ten inches, wearing a red sweat shirt. The dispatcher also advises that the individual is wanted for questioning in reference to a Ponzi Scheme. As luck would have it, she sees a person fitting that description and also carrying a backpack. Detective Alverez drives pass the individual, pulls over and exits her vehicle. As she was about to radio the dispatcher of her location and that she was stopping someone fitting that description, the young man comes to a sudden stop, looks at Alverez and runs in the other direction. Alverez gave chase and sees the young man drop the backpack and run into a nearby alley.

This young guy looked like Jesse Owens as he turned the corner. All she saw was ass and elbows as he sprinted down the alley. There was no way that she was going to catch him so she stopped and picked up the backpack. She was out of breath and ready to puke. There's a certain point in every cop's life when he or she realizes that chasing the bad guy down on foot was no longer an option. This was her day of recognition. Father time waits for no one and never loses a battle. But if you are wise, you can always learn from Father Time. What she should have done was to radio the dispatcher the particulars and ask for back up. No matter how fast the bad guy is, he can't outrun a car or the radio. And when the bad guy's tired, a young officer can chase him down while you direct the whole scenario. You should always learn from your mistakes. It's called smart policing. If you're gonna make mistakes, you might as well learn from them.

Alverez slowly walked back to her car and tossed the backpack onto the passenger seat. After catching her breath, she did what she should have done at the start of the chase. She notified the dispatcher that she had a subject fitting the description of the lookout and that she had given chase. She let the dispatcher know that the subject was last seen heading east in the alley between O and P Streets, Northwest. "No need for backup, last seen!" As she gained her composure, she remembered the backpack. She grabbed it, placed it on her lap and opened the top flap. Her eyes lit up. "Shit!" A backpack full of money. As she rummaged through it "this has to be at least twenty-thousand dollars."

Detective Alverez was in the middle of an ethical dilemma! No one was around as she gave chase. No one saw her pick up the backpack and no one knew that it was full of money. At least no one except the guy who dropped it. The money was probably dirty and if she turned it in, the government would just be twenty-thousand dollars richer. Who would benefit from that?

Chapter Nine
No Words

Later that night, Marcus sat at home in his man cave reflecting on a multitude of issues. He thought about the case at hand, his father, his sick mother and his career. Every couple of years Marcus had to go through this process to purge himself. To shed all the baggage weighing him down.

Gina walked into the room and saw the solemn look on his face. "Hey babe, you okay" she asked? Marcus just grunted and shrugged his shoulders. "Talk to me babe. You know you always hold things in and the therapist said that it's not good for you. You need to talk about it. Even if it's about work." Marcus just stared into space for a minute or two before he began to answer her. "Where do I start" he kinda asked himself? "Just thinking about my career and all the crap I've seen over the years."

"For the most part, I can tuck it away and not let it get the best of me. I kinda turn off my emotions and just not think or talk about it. The last thing that I want to do is bring my nightmares home to you. Our home is my sanctuary and this is where I come to get away from all that filth. But tonight it just hit me like a wave. All the bodies. All the dead black men just laying in the streets for no good reason. The senselessness of it all. You see their family members trying to cross the police line to get to them. They're crying and screaming and at that very moment you can't help them. All you can do is be compassionate. In the beginning it tugs at your heart, but you have to learn to cope because the police being emotional at a homicide scene just ain't a good look. You learn very fast that you have to disassociate yourself with what you're seeing or you won't make it on the job. Your emotions will get the best of you and you will become a bumbling mess and there's no way you can do your job like that."

"You take what you see and your feelings about it and pack it away in the back of your brain. Deep, deep down so that it doesn't seep out. Over the years you pack more and more crap on top of it, until none of what you see fazes you. You become an expert at hiding your emotions. You can actually turn them off. But the problem is one day it slowly starts seeping out. Something you see or hear will trigger it and that door gets cracked and out it comes. One memory at a time. One body at a time. One emotion at a time. You find yourself at home crying about something that happened twenty years ago." "Just let it out babe, talk to me" begged Gina.

Marcus took a deep breathe "I remember the first homicide I ever responded to. A man had been set on fire. My partner and I were the first to arrive. We grabbed a blanket and smothered the fire. He was still alive. He was laying there looking up at us. Burned from his neck down, smoldering. Smoke rising from his body and the horrible smell of burning flesh. He was in so much pain that he could barely talk. He looked at me and begged me to shoot him. He wanted me to take him out of his misery. I could see in his eyes that he knew that he was going to die. I couldn't speak. Couldn't say yes or no. I had no words. I didn't know what to do. My partner radioed for an ambulance and we just waited. There was nothing that I could do to help him. I couldn't save him; couldn't give him any kind of first aid. This was way above my skill level."

"Waiting for that ambulance seemed like forever. He just kept looking at me and I could see the pain in his eyes. Then his body relaxed and he breathed a sigh of relief and then stopped breathing. His appearance changed right before my eyes. I saw him go from a living being to the dearly departed. Something about the way he looked changed. One second he looked like a real person and a split second later he looked like a mannequin. It's hard to explain, but he just didn't look real anymore. I believe at that very moment, his soul left his body. I'm not saying that I actually saw his soul leave his body, but I know it did."

"I was in disbelief over what I perceived had just happened. I couldn't hold back the tears. I started crying like a damn baby. A damn baby in uniform with a badge and a gun. At that very moment, I was incapable of doing my job. It was like I was a spectator. Just watching. Not securing the scene. Not looking for evidence. Just crying. Other officers arrived on the scene and pushed me aside. They pretended like I wasn't even there. They went about doing the job that I should have been doing. Once that shift ended, I knew then that I had to find a way to numb myself from what I was seeing on the job. Either that or resign. It had to be one or the other! That vision haunted me until I learned how to disassociate myself. I would close my eyes at night and see his face. Over the next few years I learned how to remove my feelings from what I saw and after a while very little bothered me. As long as it wasn't someone that I knew or a child, I had no feelings at all. It was just a job. That was the only way that I could survive without losing my mind."

"I made it a point not to bring that pain home to you. Not to talk about it with you. To leave death and destruction outside of our front door. Sure, I talk about people and certain situations that I find funny or irritating, but I never bring the pain home to you. I don't want to trap you in my nightmares. I try really hard to separate the job from my home life. I always looked forward to coming home to you. Leaving death and destruction behind. That's why I take a shower as soon as I get home. I wash the stink of crime right down the drain."

"I'm tired babe" he said as he laid his head in Gina's lap. She caressed his head as he began to sob.

After a few minutes, Marcus sat up and wiped his eyes. "I feel silly babe" he said. Gina shook her head no "why Marcus?" Marcus continued "I know a lot of cops that have been through worse things than me. Some have seen worse, some have been in shootings and I'm sitting here being weak." "You know better than that Marcus" said Gina. "This is exactly how you remain in that cycle. Believing that you don't have the right to feel. Thinking that your colleagues are not going through the same thing. You guys don't talk about it to each other because you think it will make you appear weak. So you hold it in and the cycle of pain goes round and round. You're smarter than this. You know that the only way to overcome PTSD is to deal with it. To talk about what you've seen. To talk about your feelings. This house is a no judgment zone and you are the strongest man that I've ever known."

They lay together on the floor and Marcus let her in. He cracked the door to his vault and let a few memories flow out. He talked for hours about some of the memories that he had suppressed and it made him feel better. It was a relief and the weight he felt seemed a little lighter. He had let out enough pain to enable himself to continue in his calling. Then he shut the door to his pain for a few more years. It was the only way that he knew to refresh his self and re-charge his battery. Now he could stand tall again and be the strong man that everybody knew him to be. With Gina's help, he could be that man.

A.D. White

Chapter Ten
Close the Door Behind You

The next morning at roll call, Detective Alverez briefed the squad on what she learned from James Poole's ex-girlfriend. Detectives Steele and Callahan felt like it was a slam dunk from there. They could put surveillance on him and catch him in the act. Sergeant Powell wasn't so sure about that "okay, he's a woman beater and he likes knives, but what's his motive for killing these women?" The lieutenant chimed in "did he have any type of relationship with any of them besides installing two of their alarm systems?" The detectives remained silent. Sergeant Powell continued "I'm not saying that he's not our guy, but I'm not totally convinced that he is."

"If he's our guy, we're really missing something" said the lieutenant. "And what's the meaning of the numbers 205 and 347?" Marcus answered "I think I figured it out Lieu." Everyone looked surprised. "Enlighten us, oh wise one" joked Logan. Marcus explained "I stayed up all night racking my brains and then I had a moment of clarity. I asked myself could the numbers represent a location, you know like longitude and latitude coordinates? That didn't work. It wasn't their alarm codes or any of their house numbers. And then it occurred to me that this guy has to be the epitome of evil and a lot of evil people try to use the bible to justify their actions."

You could hear a pin drop as they all waited for his next words. "Each homicide happened on second day of the month. The second book of the bible is Exodus. The first number left was 205. So I looked up Exodus 20, verse 5 and it stated "For I am a jealous God, visiting the iniquity of the fathers on the children. I found that interesting, so next we have the number 347. There is no 47th verse of chapter three, so I looked at the 34th chapter, verse 7, which read "He will by no means leave the guilty unpunished, visiting the iniquity of fathers on the children and on the grandchildren.""

"I get it" said Detective Callahan. "From those verses you extrapolated that these crimes were the ramifications of something their fathers did. Interesting. Their father's pejorative actions somehow caused their deaths." Logan looked at Callahan "really dude? Plain English. That's all I'm asking?" Marcus smiled "yeah, that's what I'm thinking. We need to look at each of the victim's fathers and find out what connection they have to each other. The fact that those two numbers correspond to bible verses that basically say the same thing can't be a coincidence. The killer left us a clue because he thinks we're too dumb to catch him otherwise."

Lieutenant O'Malley had a surprised look on his face, "good work Marcus. That makes a lot of sense."

"Okay, now we're cooking with grease" Sergeant Powell said with a tone of excitement. "Same assignments. Al, you find out everything you can about Sarah Murphy's father. Marcus, you have Stephanie Ross' father and Logan you've got Naomi Reed's father. Callahan, I'm giving you two assignments. First, track Mr. Poole's cell phone records. Let's see where he was on the night of each murder and then coordinate with the surveillance squad and have them begin a twenty-four hour detail on him. Okay, let's go people. We've got a killer to catch!"

Lieutenant O'Malley was encouraged by Marcus' theory. The lieutenant was sort of a pessimist so he rarely seemed content. He was always foreseeing the next problem and thinking of their solutions. Preparing himself for problems that might not even arise. But at this moment he was smelling the roses. Leaning back in his chair and just relaxing for a moment when he heard the knock at his office door. He groaned "enter." In walked Sergeant John McGuire of the Internal Affairs Division.

Internal Affairs officers have a job to do. They help stamp out police corruption, but not many police officers are ever happy to see them. It's like going to the dentist. There's a problem that they can help you with, but you know it's gonna be painful. Lieutenant O'Malley and Sergeant McGuire knew each other, but there was no love lost between them. "Why have you darkened my doorstep Sergeant?" "Nice to see you too,

Lieutenant" he answered. He continued "I need to brief you on an Integrity Check that we conducted on one of your detectives."

The lieutenant sat straight up in his chair "close the door and have a seat." We've had Detective Katelyn Alverez on our radar because of the incident with her father a few years back." Lieutenant O'Malley just looked at him with no expression. This confused the Sergeant so he expounded, "the incident when she witnessed her father taking money and kept silent about it for years. She only reported it last year because she was backed into a corner." "Oh that incident" said Lieutenant O'Malley with a tinge of sarcasm.

Sergeant McGuire continued "we set up a scenario where she encountered a young man with a bag of money. He dropped the bag and ran. The Detective was unable to catch him, so she retrieved the bag and discovered that it was full of money. Little did she know, it was twenty five thousand dollars of marked money. We wanted to see what she would do with it. Would she take some of the money and turn in the rest, or take it all." At this point Lieutenant O'Malley was no longer able to contain his enthusiasm. He didn't say a word but the expression on his face undeniably screamed "what did she do with it?"

"Much to my surprise" said Sergeant McGuire, "she turned in all of the money to the Third District Police Station and completed all the required paperwork."   "I don't know why you were surprised Sergeant. All of my detectives are honest, hard-working people." "Well, she passed this time, but I could tell by the look on your face that you weren't completely sure of the outcome." Lieutenant O'Malley again gave him that expressionless face then smiled from ear to ear and said "close the door behind you Sergeant."

A.D. White

Chapter Eleven
Stephanie Ross

The first victim was Stephanie Ross and she lived in Prince William County, Virginia, which is a suburb of Washington D.C. She was a black female and was found handcuffed to a chair in her dining room on January 2nd. She had been stabbed in the back, through her heart and out of her chest cavity. She had chloroform residue on her face, indicating that it was used to incapacitate her so she could be handcuffed before she was killed. There were no signs that she had been sexually assaulted. She was found by her mother who entered with her own key because she couldn't get in touch with her daughter for two days. The number 205 was written in blood on the bottom right corner of her first floor bathroom mirror. All the doors and windows were locked when her mother arrived and the alarm was off. The front porch light bulb was broken with the base of the bulb still inserted into the socket.

Marcus talked to her mother and found out that Stephanie was thirty years old and was a manager at a local gym. She wasn't dating anyone at the time of her death and hadn't had a steady boyfriend for a few years. Even though she worked at the gym, she was an aspiring writer. She was working on her first book which was a love story. Her co-workers said that she seemed to be very happy and there was no drama in her life.

Stephanie was tall, dark skinned with an athletic build. Good looking by most standards. She had taken a few self-defense courses that were offered at the gym that she managed so it appeared she could handle herself physically.

Her father's name was Ben Ross and he died two years ago from a heart attack. Stephanie was the apple of his eye and could do no wrong in his sight. She thought the same of him and was definitely a daddy's girl. Everyone around him knew about his daughter, because he constantly talked about Stephanie. He was a proud father and would do anything for his daughter. At the time of his death, Ben Ross worked at Abrams Armored Carriers. He was a manager there but started out as a driver. He worked there for twenty years. Ben had no criminal record and his wife didn't know of any connection he could have had to his daughter's murder.

Chapter Twelve
Naomi Reed

The second victim was Naomi Reed and she lived in Montgomery County, Maryland, which is a suburb of Washington D.C. She was a white female and was found handcuffed and lying face down in her living room on March 2nd. She had been stabbed in the back, through her heart and out of her chest cavity. She also had chloroform residue on her face, indicating that her murderer incapacitated her, before handcuffing her. As was the case with Stephanie Ross. There were no signs that Naomi had been sexually assaulted either.

Naomi lived on the first floor of an apartment building and was found by one of the employees of her rental office after a noise complaint. Her music was playing very loudly for hours and one of her neighbors called the rental office to make a complaint. The property manager entered with a key through the locked front door. The back door and all the windows were locked. There was no alarm system installed. The number 347 was written in blood on the bottom right corner of the mirror in her bedroom bathroom. The front porch light bulb of the building was broken with the base of the bulb still inserted into the socket.

Logan talked to her mother and found out that she was twenty-eight years old and was an elementary school teacher. She was of average height with long blonde hair and a shapely figure. Her best feature was her smile which seemed to attract a hoard of men. She complained to her mother that she was constantly being approached by men and women everywhere she went. It seemed as though her beauty was a hindrance to her. Her co-workers described her as a happy person but sort of an introvert. She was friendly but reserved and was not dating at the time of her death, although her options were plenty. She liked to work out and was a member of the same gym that Stephanie Ross managed, but frequented a different location.

Naomi's father was Carter Reed. He had a stroke one year ago and was living in an inpatient rehabilitation facility. He lost his ability to speak and had little movement throughout his body. Even though he was retired, it was discovered that some years earlier he worked at the same Armored Car Carrier that Ben Ross worked at. He had also been a driver and had no criminal record.

Chapter Thirteen
Sarah Murphy

The third victim was Sarah Murphy and she lived in the Fort Lincoln neighborhood of D.C. She was a white female and was found handcuffed to her bed on May 2nd. Like the others, she had been stabbed in the back, through her heart and out of her chest cavity. She also had chloroform residue on her face. There were no signs of a sexual assault. She was found by police who received a call stating that there was a dead woman at that location.

The number 347 was written in blood on the bottom right corner of her first floor bathroom. All the doors and windows were locked when the police arrived and the alarm was not set. The front porch light bulb was broken with the base of the bulb still inserted into the socket.

Detective Alverez talked to her mother. Sarah had a slightly difficult life. She experimented with drugs for a few years before changing her life. She worked at a credit union and went back to school to get her bachelor's degree. By all standards she was doing well and was happy with her new found life.

Sarah's father's name was James Murphy. James mysteriously disappeared from his daughter's life about two years ago. A check of James record revealed that he had been arrested for robbery when he was a juvenile but his arrest record had been sealed. That's probably why he was able to get a job at the same Armored Car Carrier that Ben Ross and Carter Reed worked at.

Chapter Fourteen
Verbal Dyslexia

The inquiry into each of the victim's fathers yielded a major clue and a common denominator. At one time or another, they all worked for Abrams Armored Carriers. So as you can imagine, that was the next stop for Marcus and Logan. Callahan was on the way to Mr. Poole's cell phone carrier to track his whereabouts during the time periods of the three murders. He was still a suspect!

The three of them walked out of Headquarters and down the street to their perspective cars. Marcus took a deep breath "ah, smells like rain" he said. Logan never missing a moment to offer his retort "was it the dark clouds that tipped you off Detective" as he smiled to signal his pleasure. "I didn't say that it looked like rain, I said it smelled like rain. You don't smell that in the air?" "All I smell is exhaust fumes and crime" answered Logan. Marcus fired back "when you learn how to use your five senses you'll become a better detective."

"All I need is common sense" said Logan. "We both know that common sense ain't that common" added Callahan. "And before you ask, that's not one of the five senses" he added. Logan mumbled something incoherent. "Okay Sensei, give me an example of how your senses make you a better detective." Marcus thought for a second, then said "You hear a loud bang and you're not sure if it was a gunshot or a car backfiring. As you investigate, you smell gun powder. You heard the bang, you smell the gunpowder then you see a blood trail. Its' a basic example, but you just used three of your senses to tell you that someone's been shot." "Sounds like common sense to me" Logan joked. "The last two are touch and taste" said Callahan. "We all know what I use those for" said Logan. "Wow, your lack of evolution is astonishing" joked Callahan. "Thank you" responded Logan. "It wasn't a compliment" said Marcus. "So says you Detective Rose." "I don't even know why I try" Marcus shook his head. "Get in the car Logan, and no you can't drive." "I don't want to drive" responded Logan. "Always gotta get the last word huh?"

Callahan was amused by their verbal exchange and asked "are you two secretly married?" Logan laughed and said "yeah, and he's the girl" as he pointed to Marcus. Just then an old C.I. (Confidential Informant) of Logan's walked up and said "if it ain't Black Ice" (referring to Logan). Logan earned that nickname by his peers because he was tall, dark and considered to be cool. Thus, Black Ice.

"Tony Talk A lot, I haven't seen you in years" responded Logan. "Yeah man, same day, different shit. I trip took a little" he said. Marcus and Callahan looked at each other thoroughly confused. Logan laughed and introduced them. "Tony has what you might call...verbal dyslexia. Instead of letters of a word being turned around, his words in a sentence get turned around. What he said was "I took a little trip. And by trip, do you mean to D.C. Jail?" "You always could understand me" laughed Tony.

Callahan mumbled "the fact that you understand him says a lot about you." "I've got it all together now though. I knew sooner or later that our cross would paths. If you want I can car your drive for you." Marcus looked at him and said "Nah, we good. I wanna get there safely." Tony continued to talk about nothing for a few minutes before Callahan interrupted "your name should be Loquacious Tony. I think it's very descriptive of you." "Loquacious huh...yeah I like that." Marcus got into their car as Logan said "Okay Tony, we gotta bounce, but it was good seeing you brotha."

Tony had another annoying quality. Once he started a conversation with you, it was hard to get away from him. His excessive talking seemed to hold you hostage, making it hard to end the conversation and walk away. "Are you guys working on that Boogey Man case? I can keep my street to the ears if you guys need some info." "Yeah, you do that Tony. Let me know what you come up with" said Logan as he quickly got into their vehicle, leaving Callahan on an island by himself. As Callahan quickly started to walk away, he offered a bit of advice for Tony. "You know your incessant talking could

be a sign of ADHD. You should get that checked out."
"Yeah man, do that I might" was his response.

As Marcus and Logan drove away, Marcus looked at Logan and said "I know it's probably not a word, but Tony is Stupider than you."   For once, Logan didn't respond. He just laughed.

Chapter Fifteen
Abrams Armored Carriers

Marcus and Logan arrived at Abrams Armored Carriers. A red bricked building with an old sign above the front door bearing its name. The front door was chipping and in desperate need of fresh paint. Just looking at it made Marcus want to wash his hands. So he did with his pocket sanitizer just after entering the building. The front counter was made of wood and covered with dust. If this business was profitable, it definitely didn't reflect in its appearance Marcus thought to himself.

Now we all know that Marcus has an obsession with germs, so when the older lady behind the front desk started violently coughing without covering her mouth, Marcus took a step back and allowed Logan to lead. In Marcus' mind, he could see the germs floating in the air as she wiped her mouth with her right hand. She looked as if she was in her sixties, short, white haired with disheveled clothing. She got up, adjusted her dress and asked with a southern drawl "can I help ya'll?"

Now, Logan knew Marcus well. Better than anyone else with the exception of his wife Gina. He was more than familiar with Marcus' phobia of germs and knew that he was squirming in his own skin just being in that dirty building. But when that woman coughed into the air and wiped her mouth with her hands, Logan was dying inside with laughter. Logan introduced himself and Marcus while showing her his credentials. "I'm Milly, how you guys doing" she said as she extended her right hand to Marcus. Marcus didn't want to be rude, but there was no damn way he was shaking her hand so Logan interceded by telling her why they were there while trying not to laugh.

"We need some information on three of your past employees ma'am. And if possible, we would love to talk to anyone who worked with them." "Whatcha need that for" she asked? "It's part of a murder investigation ma'am" responded Logan. "Murder" she said with a shocked tone. "You gonna need a warrant for that sweetie." Marcus just couldn't take it any longer "you know what ma'am? This place is filthy and I'm pretty sure that it is a health hazard to your employees and anybody who sets foot in this unsanitary excuse for an office. You know, the health department doesn't just deal with food establishments. They also look into places of business that may jeopardize the well-being of its employees. I can have an inspector down here within the hour and I can bet you pennies to a dollar that you'll be closed down until this place has been renovated."

That obviously offended Milly as she responded "don't have a hissy fit. Let me call the owner" as she went into the back office. Logan looked at Marcus, grinned and asked "pennies to a dollar? What the hell was that?" Marcus smiled "I don't know man. Since this place is so dirty, it was fitting that I pulled that one right out of you know where." They both laughed. They could hear Milly on the phone complaining to someone about their inquiry. She came back to the counter and attempted to hand Marcus a business card "here, this is the owner and he's just pickled to talk to ya." Marcus just looked at the card. Again, there was no damn way that he was going to take that card from her germ riddled hand. Logan reached over and took the card "thank you ma'am, you have been a great help to us. May your future be bright and all your dreams come true." "Ah-ha" she responded as she glared at Marcus.

As they left the building, Logan stated "she didn't even ask who the employees were. Oh and uh, let me see your hand sanitizer. Marcus laughed and pulled it out and squirted some on Logan's hands as he held them out like a child receiving candy. They got into their vehicle and looked at the business card. Samuel Abrams was the owner and CEO of the company. "I've heard of him" Marcus remarked, then dialed his number and told him of their desire to obtain information on three of his past employees. Mr. Abrams told him that his office was in his home and he would give them any information that they needed if they wanted to come by.

As they drove through Georgetown, Logan remarked how they don't get to see this part of the city much. It was a pleasure just driving through such an historic place with high class stores and expensive homes. It even smelled differently. Today, they truly took time to smell the roses and appreciate the city that Marcus grew up in. While it's hard for most people to see the forest for the trees, it's twice as hard for a police detective to see the beauty of D.C. through the crime.

Abrams lived on 29th Street in the Georgetown section of D.C. They pulled onto the street and admired all the gated houses, circular drive ways and big yards. "This is gonna be me one day" Logan joked. "Speak it into existence my brotha. From your mouth to God's ears." They pulled up to the gate and pressed the buzzer. The gate opened immediately as if Mr. Abrams had been waiting for their arrival. They walked up a few stairs and knocked on the door using a very large knocker. The door opened and there stood Samuel Abrams, sophisticated looking, a little over six feet tall, 65 years old with salt and pepper hair. Well groomed, dressed in black slacks and a white shirt, no tie. You could tell that he worked out just by his appearance. He apparently had the secret to aging gracefully and everything about him spelled e-x-p-e-n-s-i-v-e.

"Hello detectives; I'm Samuel Abrams. How can I be of assistance to you," he asked? "I'm Detective Rose and this is my partner Detective Steele. May we come in" Marcus asked? "Certainly," he responded. "Let's talk in my office," as he closed the door, turned around and walked down the hall with Marcus and Logan following. His business office and home office were like night and day. Large oak desk with a matching leather chair. Built in book shelves to match. A large painting of himself on the wall. Impressed by his vast book collection, Marcus asked "have you read all these books sir?" "Every last one of them" he responded.   "Impressive" Marcus remarked.

"Have a seat gentlemen" as he pointed to two chairs sitting across from his desk. Marcus got the feeling that the chairs had been placed there just for this moment. "Who are the employees that you need information about" Mr. Abrams asked. "Ben Ross, Carter Reed and James Murphy" answered Marcus.

"Milly tells me that the information you need is part of a murder investigation?" Marcus really didn't want to answer that question or give him too much information, but nodded yes. "The information could help or may not be relevant to our investigation at all" Marcus replied. "Really? I know that you're time is valuable and even though I just met you, you don't strike me as a frivolous person. I'm sure that the information that you require is of far greater importance than you're letting on. Nevertheless, I would be happy to help in any way that I can."

Marcus and Logan had worked with each other for so long that at times they could read each other's minds with just a glance. They looked at each other as to say "he's a real slick talker. This is going to be very interesting." Mr. Abrams continued "I'm very familiar with these three men. They have caused me a lot of distress in the past." "Really, how so?" Marcus asked.

Samuel Abrams leaned back in his chair and began to take them on a long winding story of significant proportions. He told them a story that dated back to the year 2005 that involved four friends. Ben Ross was a supervisor. Carter Reed and James Murphy were drivers. The fourth friend was Sebastian Eckert who was the accountant for the company. The four of them were as thick as thieves. (Pun intended) James Murphy was the master mind of the group and seemed to have great influence over the others. James, with the help of the others, devised a plan to steal five million dollars from one of the armored cars that he and Carter were driving. Ben Ross and Sebastian Eckert knew all the intimate details of when a very large shipment of money would be picked up. The shipment was much larger than their normal collection and they referred to it as the "Mother Load."

Sebastian and Benn Ross devised a plan where as James Murphy and Carter Reed would collect a total of ten million dollars from two banks but all the paperwork would indicate that only five million had been collected, leaving five million dollars unaccounted for and at their disposal. Sebastian was the book worm and assured everyone that it could be done. The others really didn't fully understand how Sebastian could manipulate the paperwork, but they trusted that he was just that clever.

Trusting in a plan that they didn't fully understand was their first mistake and actually going through with the plan was their second. The men split up the money four ways. When it was discovered that five million dollars was missing, James Murphy, Carter Reed and Ben Ross flipped on Sebastian Eckert faster than lies leaving a politicians lips. They sang like the O'Jays. They blamed the entire plot on Sebastian Eckert and eagerly offered to testify against him. In exchange for their cooperation, the three of them were not charged. Sebastian Eckert made a deal and plead guilty to robbery and conspiracy to commit robbery. It was if he had done it all by himself. He was sentenced to twenty years in jail and would be eligible for parole after ten.

Samuel Abrams pulled a few strings and the whole plot received very little media attention. What little was reported was inaccurate saving Abrams Armored Carriers the embarrassment of this whole fiasco. This story blew Marcus and Logan away. They were exhausted just from listening to this tale. This information gave their investigation a whole new turn. Finding out the whereabouts of Sebastian Eckert was priority number one.

A.D. White

Chapter Sixteen
Samuel Abrams

Samuel Abrams bore some looking into. He was an interesting guy with more to him than meets the eye. Detective Callahan did what he does best, background checks or in laymen's terms, digging up your dirt. It was his knack because he was a curious guy by nature. Some would call it nosey, but that's only when you do it without being paid! He'd type up the info and place it in a dossier which went to the lieutenant for his review, then to the squad.

Samuel Abrams' dossier revealed that he was six feet one inches tall, 65 years old with salt and pepper hair. Well educated with a Master degree in Psychology from Old Dominion University in Norfolk, Virginia. Actually practiced his craft for ten years before his father died and left him the business (Abrams Armored Carriers). His father, John Abrams was a self-made man. Had a business degree and made his money in the stock market. He was investigated several times for insider trading but was never charged. He accumulated a wealth of thirty million dollars which his only child inherited. He was known as a ruthless business man. Samuel idolized his father.

Samuel trained in the martial art of Jiu Jitsu and competed in mix martial arts for a few years. Although business was his main priority, staying in shape and fighting was his second love. He was smart and calculating, never overlooking a chance to advance his agenda. He never married and didn't have any children. He was also known to be a ruthless business man just like daddy.

Chapter Seventeen
Sebastian Eckert

Marcus and the team were excited and encouraged by the emergence of Sebastian Eckert as a suspect. They felt they were on the right track. The next step was to find out everything they could about him and his whereabouts. Detective Callahan put together the dossier. After a day or so, the Professor as they called him, dug up all that he could about Sebastian Eckert. There were a lot of unknowns concerning Sebastian, but he did find out that Sebastian was an orphan. His parents died in a fire when he was eight years old.

He bounced around to different foster homes until he left the system at age eighteen never finding a family to adopt him. This left him with a lifelong feeling of rejection and insecurity. Despite his circumstances, he excelled in academia. A natural with numbers which at times seemed to be his only friend. He was your classic nerd, right down to his thick black framed glasses. When he was picked on at school he reverted into his own world and fantasized about elaborate ways to extract revenge on his oppressors.

An introvert of sorts which made it hard for others to get to know him. He was a watcher. Said very little

99

but observed everything. Because of this, when he did make a friend, he was easily influenced by them. He mimicked the people he was around. He might have thought that it was the only way that he could gain the acceptance of others. It was hard to tell who the real Sebastian Eckert was.

Due to his high IQ, he was awarded several academic scholarships. He accepted the one from Columbia University in New York and majored in accounting. Then got his MBA from Stanford University. Even though he was great at his job, because of his awkwardness, he bounced around from job to job and state to state. Even though Sebastian was awkward at personal relationships, he somehow managed to father a daughter in California. His employment tour around the country led him to Washington D.C. and eventually to Abrams Armored Carriers where he met the crew. Ben Ross, Carter Reed and James Murphy. He started hanging out with them which meant drinking after work at the local bar called the Drunken Skunk.

The crew was intrigued by Sebastian. They tried to figure him out, which was the subject of many conversations when he wasn't around. During this time, the crew noticed that alcohol had very little effect on him. No matter how much he drank, he never got drunk. They admired that about him and accepted him even though he didn't talk much. He was like their own little party trick. He could drink anyone under the table which won them a few bets at the bar. What no one knew was that Sebastian's body produced a more than usual amount of Acetaldehyde Dehydrogenase. An enzyme that breaks down alcohol in the body. It's a very rare condition and the reason that alcohol had very little effect on him. It ingratiated him with the crew and he became one of them. For the very first time, Sebastian felt accepted and he would do anything to continue fitting in.

After their joint crime venture went awry and the crew betrayed Sebastian, as criminals often do, he was left full of rage. He couldn't believe that they talked him into this idiotic plan but when their backs were up against the wall, they threw him under the bus. Then backed up over him. He didn't take betrayal well.

Much to everyone's surprise, he adapted to the prison life. Became institutionalized with a purpose, helping other inmates with their appeals and teaching math as part of the prison GED program. A model inmate. But at night he spent his time dreaming of ways to repay his so called friends for stabbing him in the back. Sebastian spent eleven years in jail. Due to his chameleon like adaptation, he was paroled in 2016. After his parole, he quietly took up residence in a cabin in the woods of Olney, Maryland. About twenty miles north of Washington, D.C. in a secluded area.

Eighteen months later, he moved into an up and coming section of D.C. in the waterfront district near the baseball stadium. He apparently had a wealth of money that no one knew about. It made the team wonder if he somehow managed to keep some of that stolen money.

Chapter Eighteen
Purpose and a Little Patience

Detectives Callahan and Alverez made a surprise visit to his condo to escort him to the homicide branch for an interview. Sebastian's building was so new it smelled like freshly poured concrete. "How can he afford this," Alverez wondered? "For a convict, he sure bounced back quickly" stated Callahan. They walked by the concierge on the way to the elevators. The concierge jumped up and asked "can I help you two?" Detective Alverez flashed her credentials and said "no, we got this."

The concierge was clueless as he informed them that he couldn't let them by without notifying the person that they were here to see. Alverez kinda smiled and shook her head as they proceeded to the elevators. They exited the elevator on the third floor and proceeded to apartment 347 and knocked on the door. A loud forceful knock. The door opened and there stood Sebastian Eckert. All five foot four inches of him. Wearing a pair of black khakis with a white dress shirt buttoned up all the way to the neck. Black rimmed eye glasses and clean shaven. He was so short they could see the bald spot in the middle of his head.

"Are you Sebastian Eckert" asked Callahan? "I am" he responded. "I'm Detective Callahan and this is

Detective Alverez of the D.C. Police Department. We'd like for you to come down to our office and answer a few questions." Sebastian had an indifferent look on his face and he responded, "of course, I've been expecting you" as he walked out of his front door and closed it behind him. He didn't ask what this was about or why they wanted to speak to him. He knew what it was about and wanted them to know that he wasn't fazed about it at all. No worries in the world. It was as though he was playing mind games with them from the very start.

The ride to their office was eerie. No one talked and Sebastian just glared out the window as they hurried on their way. An uncomfortable silence filled the air. They arrived and put him in interview room 3. Marcus and Logan were at their desks and watched them walk by as Sebastian leered at them. The anticipation was brewing as this interview had the air of a prize fight. Lieutenant O'Malley, Sergeant Powell, Detectives Callahan and Alverez were all in the observation deck waiting to see Marcus square off with their number one suspect. All they needed now was a bucket of popcorn for the main event.

As usual, Marcus let his suspect sit in the interview room for about twenty minutes before he went in. He liked for them to marinate a bit before cooking them. Marcus and Logan entered the room and closed the door behind them. Marcus flipped the switch on the wall and asked "you don't mind if we record this, do you?" "As you wish" responded Sebastian. Marcus and Logan sat down beside each other with Sebastian on the other side of the table. Marcus reached inside of his jacket pocket and removed his hand sanitizer. He looked at Logan and raised his hand holding the sanitizer as to ask if Logan wanted some. Logan responded "Nah, I'm good." Marcus squirted some on his hand and rubbed them together vigorously.

Marcus: My name is Detective Marcus Rose and this is my partner, Detective Logan Steele. We'd like to ask you a few questions if you don't mind.

Sebastian: I'm at your disposal detectives.

Marcus: You're not in the least curious about what we'd like to talk about?

Sebastian: Seeing that the placard on the front door said Homicide, I assume that it's about a death.

Marcus: You assumed correctly Mr. Eckert.

Sebastian: Please, call me Sebastian.

Marcus: Do you know Ben Ross, Carter Reed and James Murphy?

Sebastian: I do. We used to work together and at one time we were friends. I also assume that you already knew that though.

Marcus: You did more than work together Sebastian. I'm told that you were all co-conspirators in a crime. A crime in which you went to prison for and they got a slap on the wrist. I guess there's no honor among thieves.

Sebastian: Is that a question detective?

Marcus: How'd that make you feel?

Sebastian: Well Dr. Phil (sarcastically) I wasn't happy about it.

Marcus: If my so called friends flipped on me and I went to jail for something that we all did, I'd be very angry.

Sebastian: Okay detective, I'll bite. I was angry.

Marcus: Angry enough to kill?

Sebastian: Of course not, all I wanted was justice.

Marcus: Justice or revenge?

Sebastian: Isn't this where you're supposed to read me my rights?

Logan: It sure is. You have the right to remain silent. You are not required to say anything to us at any time or to answer any questions. Anything you say can be used against you in court. You have the right to talk to a lawyer for advice before we question you and to have him with you during questioning. If you cannot afford a lawyer, one will be provided for you. Do you understand these rights?

Sebastian: I do.

Logan: Do you want a lawyer?

Sebastian: No, not at this time, but I do reserve the right to change my mind.

Marcus: Did your former friends betrayal make you angry enough to kill?

Sebastian: As far as I know detective, James, Carter and Ben are alive. Who's dead (he asked with an evil grin)?

Marcus: Their daughters Sebastian. Each of your co-conspirators had daughters that were killed.

Sebastian: Why would I kill their daughter's detective?

Marcus: Listen, I'm sorry for your loss.

(Sebastian just stared at Marcus)

Marcus: Your daughter Megan passed away while you were in prison and the warden wouldn't even let you attend her funeral.

Sebastian: You people always try to invoke emotion as a tool.

That got a visible rise out of Logan as it was meant to do.

Logan: You people?

Sebastian: (laughed) Don't get your panties in a bunch detective. I'm referring to you cops. If you think that I'm going to sit here and pour my heart out to you, you're wrong. You think that by mentioning my daughter it will bring out rage or maybe guilt. I don't do either. They're both wasted emotions.

Marcus: Are you saying that you don't feel guilt Sebastian?

Sebastian: Guilt is a weakness detective. I don't have any weaknesses.

Marcus: Wow!

Sebastian: You seem puzzled by me detective.

Marcus: (Chuckles) I'm just as puzzled by you as a mechanic would be over a pair of worn out brakes. It's really not hard to figure you out.

Sebastian: So you think that you have me figured out, huh? Care to share your theory? Hypothetically of course.

Marcus: (Squirts some sanitizer on his hands as he begins) I think you're either a psychopath or a sociopath.

Sebastian: Psychopath?

Marcus: Yeah, psychopath. To do what you've done, you'd have to be one or the other.

Sebastian: You still haven't told me what I've done. Hypothetically that is!

Marcus: After your so called friends stabbed you in the back and sent you to prison, you sat in prison for eleven years plotting your revenge. You appeared to be the model prisoner cause they never would have let you out if they'd known what was in store for the people that wronged you.

Sebastian: Go on detective, this sounds riveting.

Marcus: When you got out, you killed their daughters. I think that you broke into their homes in the morning after each of them left for work. You disabled their security alarms by cutting the phone lines. Probably learned that in prison. Being the patient psychopath that you are, you waited all day in their homes until they returned. You waited until they were relaxed and then you made your move.

(Sebastian looked unimpressed with Marcus' story)

Marcus: Where were you on February 2nd of this year?
Sebastian: At home by myself.

Marcus: How about on April 2nd of this year?

Sebastian: At home by myself.

Logan: Let me guess. On July 2nd of this year you were probably home by yourself also.

Sebastian: I can tell that you're a great detective (he said with a smirk on his face).

Marcus: Seeing that your stature is very small and you don't look like you could bust a grape, you came up behind those women and used chloroform to incapacitate them. It didn't knock them completely out, but it did disable them enough for you to handcuff them. At which time you drove a knife through their backs and into their hearts probably after charming them with your sparkling personality. Just the way that their fathers did you metaphorically.

(Sebastian had a gleam in his eyes. Marcus knew that he was right on track. Sebastian almost looked pleased that he had a formidable foe. He was impressed that Marcus had figured it out)

Marcus: Their fathers stabbed you in the back when they turned on you, which broke your heart and caused you to be handcuffed and sent to prison. Your daughter died while you were locked up, so you decided to take their daughters away also. You wanted them to feel the same pain that they caused you.

Sebastian: Why wouldn't I just kill them?

Marcus: Because you wanted them to suffer just as you did. You wanted them to live with the consequences of their actions and their children to pay for the sins of their fathers.

Logan: The number 205 or 347 was written in blood at each crime scene. Once we figured out the significance of those numbers, we established your motive.

(Marcus looked at Logan as to say "we". Logan smiled because he knew exactly what Marcus was thinking.)

Sebastian: What do those numbers mean (as if he didn't know)?

Marcus: First of all, each murder occurred on the second day of the month which led me to the second book of the bible, Exodus. The number 205 stood for the twentieth chapter and the fifth verse which states something to the effect "I am a jealous God, visiting the iniquity of the fathers on the children."

(Sebastian fought to hold back his grin as to say "well done detective")

Marcus: The other number was 347, which led us to the thirty fourth chapter and seventh verse of Exodus, which states something to the effect of "yet He will by no means leave the guilty unpunished, visiting the iniquity of the fathers on the children."

Logan: Bottom line, you tried to play God and punish their daughters for their father's perceived sins.

Sebastian: Wow, that's some tale you've spun there detective. I'm impressed with your imagination. Figuring it out is one thing, but proving it is another, hypothetically speaking.

Logan: Who says we can't prove it?

Sebastian: If you could prove your theory, I'd be in handcuffs right now!

Marcus: In due time Sebastian. In due time. You're not as smart as you think you are. You've made mistakes!

Sebastian: I'm curious detective. Why would one have to be a psychopath to carry out such a scheme?

Marcus: Whoever did this would have to be cold and calculating. Meticulous and carefully planning every move. He probably watched those women for weeks before putting his plan into action. He sat there and waited for those woman without any fear of being caught or the consequences of his actions, thus feeling no guilt. You yourself said that guilt was a wasted emotion.

Logan raises his hand to sarcastically join the conversation. Marcus feeling dirty after that exchange cleans his hands again.

Logan: Another reason why the culprit had to be a psychopath is the blood.

Sebastian: The blood?

Logan: The killer stabbed them in a way that would produce a large amount of blood. He's not turned off at the sight of blood the way most people would be. He probably likes it. Gives him a hard on, so to speak.

Sebastian: You know, some people believe that the sight of blood has a soothing quality and a somewhat pleasing aroma.

Marcus: Really?

Sebastian: It has a metallic fragrance to it (As he breathed in heavily and smiled).

Marcus: I know that this was all hypothetical because you would have to be one sick puppy to fit that description.

Sebastian: People judge what they don't understand!

Marcus: Sooner or later you'll slip up. You might even want to get caught. (Marcus looks into his eyes for a reaction but sees none).

Sebastian: You think you're pretty smart, don't you detective?

Marcus: (Marcus shakes his head no) I'm just good at reading people.

Sebastian: I'm pretty good at reading people also. Let me take a stab at you. Hypothetically, that is.

Marcus: Go ahead, amuse me.

Sebastian: Don't get me wrong, I'm not judging you. Like I said, people judge what they don't understand. You have your own set of issues detective. Or shall we call them idiosyncrasies.

Marcus: (leans back in his chair and starts playing with the hairs on his chin)

Sebastian: I notice that you clean your hands a lot with that hand sanitizer. You're a germaphobe which is a type of Obsessive Compulsive Disorder. No one is really sure what causes it. My guess is that it stems from something in your childhood. Most likely, mommy or daddy issues. I'm guessing it was daddy.

Marcus: All right, I've grown tired of your babbling. I don't think that you have the stones to carry out what we've talked about anyway.

Sebastian: You'd be surprised what a person could do with a purpose and a little patience when properly motivated!

Marcus: Did you kill those women?

Sebastian: I did not. I'm not a violent man detective, but I think things into existence which is not a crime.

That statement took Marcus by surprise.

Marcus: Are you saying that simply by thinking of a scenario, you can cause it to happen?

Sebastian didn't answer that question; he just looked at Marcus and Logan with a purposeful glare.

Marcus: What do you do for a living these days Sebastian?

Sebastian: I'm currently on a sabbatical detective.

Marcus: I didn't know that you were a religious man. But then again, even the devil knows the bible! They tell me he uses it against his victims to justify his actions.

Sebastian: Are you calling me the devil?

Marcus: No, you're too short to be the devil, but there is something very evil about you.

Sebastian: There you go judging me again detective. I've grown tired of this and would like to leave. Am I under arrest?

Logan: No, not at this time. You're free to go. Oh, I forgot to tell you that we just executed a search warrant on your condo Sebastian.

Sebastian suddenly looked bothered. His eyelids started to flicker involuntarily. Marcus' guess was that the thought of strangers rummaging through Sebastian's belongings was disturbing to him.

Sebastian: (Stood up) Thanks for that trip down memory lane. I won't be needing a ride back from you. I'll just catch an Uber.

Marcus and Logan stood up as Sebastian walked out. They all gathered in the office to have a conference. "He damn near admitted that he did it" said Logan. "We all know that he did it, all the pieces fit right into place. Now we have to prove it without a doubt" said Lieutenant O'Malley. "Was he creepy or what" asked Alverez as she shivered? "Did you see the look on his face when he talked about blood" commented Callahan? "Yeah, the same way a fat kid talks about food" said Marcus. They all got a laugh out of that in the midst of this jarring interview.

Marcus had a determined look on his face "We'll get him. It's only a matter of time. He knows we're on to him now and if I'm reading him right, he's gonna take this as a challenge. This is where he slips up." "That was a fine job of verbal sparring there Marcus" said Sergeant Powell. Marcus replied "I'm just getting started Sarge." Then Sergeant Powell said something very profound which impressed the group "nothing is impossible to the willing mind." Then he messed it up by mumbling something no one understood right after that. Marcus tossed Logan the car keys "let's go and put this plan into action."

Chapter Nineteen
Cabin in the Woods

Marcus was spot on. Knowing that the police were searching his condo rattled Sebastian. He quickly summoned an Uber and went directly home. As he got to his front door, a man who appeared to be a maintenance worker had just finished repairing the lock to his door. "The police just left" said the maintenance guy. "They really messed up your place." "What were they looking for," Sebastian thought out loud, not really expecting a response. "I heard them say something about chlorine or something like that" the maintenance man responded. Sebastian thought to himself "chlorine, that doesn't make sense. That idiot must mean chloroform!" Then he rushed back downstairs while making a phone call.

During the background check on Sebastian Eckert, Detective Callahan uncovered his secluded cabin in the woods. This is most likely where Sebastian's plans were birthed. Detectives had just searched the cabin but found nothing significant. But Sebastian didn't know that. Marcus' plan was a long shot, but they felt they had nothing to lose. The maintenance worker at Sebastian's place was actually a detective. They wanted Sebastian to know that they were trying to connect him with the purchase or possession of chloroform, which is a restricted drug. Marcus surmised that the chloroform as well as any other implements of Sebastian's crime had to be stored at his cabin at one time or another. The problem was Marcus and his team didn't have any direct evidence linking Sebastian to the crime. Everything they had up until this point was circumstantial and they knew it wasn't enough to secure a conviction.

Marcus was betting that Sebastian would rush there just to make sure that he hadn't left any evidence behind. Marcus had a bottle of chloroform that had been borrowed from the FBI. He planned on telling Sebastian that it had been found at the cabin in hopes that he would lose his cool and say something incriminating.

As the sun began to set, Marcus waited inside the cabin for Sebastian's arrival. Detective's Steele, Callahan and Alverez along with Sergeant Powell were positioned at different points in the woods that surrounded the cabin. After an hour had passed, a dark compact car slowly drove up the long driveway to the cabin. It pulled off the side of the road, about 100 yards from the cabin and Sebastian got out of the vehicle. Sergeant Powell quietly radioed Marcus what they were seeing. As he slowly approached the cabin, Sebastian visually searched the tree line for anything out of the ordinary.

Just by happenstance, he saw a flicker of light reflect off one of the detective's radio, so he turned around and started running back to the car. "I think he made us. Move in," ordered Sergeant Powell. The detectives converged on Sebastian as he fell down in a panic. He even ran like a nerd. Filled with disappointment, Marcus got up and started walking towards the door when he heard someone enter the back door of the cabin. He didn't radio the detectives outside for fear that he would be heard. Marcus froze as Samuel Abrams walked into the living room with gun in hand. "Well, well, well, if it isn't Detective Rose" he said with genuine surprise. "It all makes sense now" said Marcus. Samuel Abrams waived the gun at Marcus "sit detective and don't even think about reaching for your gun or radio."

At this very moment, Marcus had to make a decision. Do I go for my gun or not? His gun is already out, am I fast enough to draw mine before he can shoot me? Marcus didn't like those odds, so he decided to stall Samuel Abrams. Sooner or later when one of the other detectives noticed that Marcus hadn't come outside, they would come inside looking for him.

"I should have known that you were involved in this" said Marcus. "I don't know how I didn't see it." "Yep, you sure should have detective. You weren't smart enough to catch me and Sebastian Eckert wasn't smart enough to have pulled this off by himself. He's what I call a useful idiot," as he flashed a cunning grin. "You were his puppet master the whole time" Marcus commented. Samuel and Marcus could see out the window as the detectives put Sebastian in their vehicle and drove away. "Looks like they were so excited to arrest the boogey man that they forgot about you detective" as he grinned with amusement. Samuel continued "I'm not going to give you credit for partially figuring this out. I basically spoon fed you. You figured out the clues that I left you and tracked them to Sebastian just as I wanted you to." Marcus smiled "sometimes you don't know what you don't know...until you know it." Samuel looked confused by that statement. "You'll figure it out later" chimed Marcus.

I underestimated you Mr. Abrams. I didn't realize the scope of your intelligence. You carefully crafted this entire plan" said Marcus (just to stroke his ego). Samuel Abrams sat down on the other side of the room and wanted to let Marcus know how clever he really was. At a certain point, even psychopaths want credit for their work. They want everyone to know just how smart they are. They want you to know that you've been outsmarted. You know, rub your face in it.

"I saw how Carter, James and Ben manipulated Sebastian to go along with their plan. He didn't have the stones to come up with this on his own. It's partly his fault for being willfully stupid. When they got caught, they turned on him like rabid animals. Every man for himself. No accountability. Now tell me detective, was that right?"

Marcus just hunched his shoulders. Samuel continued "then his daughter dies while he's in jail and they wouldn't even let him got to the funeral. So I decided that they should pay for their crimes. They didn't even visit him while he was locked up. He confided in me and told me that he wanted justice. I convinced him that he could determine their fate just by willing it. Kinda like my own Jedi mind trick" he said with pleasure. We talked about how they would suffer if their children had to pay for their crimes. There has to be consequences detective or the world will run amuck" he said as he began to get agitated.

"Who appointed you God" asked Marcus? Samuel responded "circumstance required that I take action detective. If that's playing God, then so be it! I read the bible. An eye for an eye and a tooth for a tooth. "Really" said Marcus. "You're gonna defend the indefensible?" "Chaos rules when good men do nothing detective. You should know that. You do it every day in your job. You step in and make people pay for their crimes." Marcus responded "no, I arrest people for their crimes and a court of law punishes them. I don't determine their fate. I don't play God."

"Well, your system didn't work detective. Ben, James and Carter didn't pay for their crimes, Sebastian paid the price. He came up with the plan and I put it into action. He couldn't actually kill anyone, so I did. This fool actually thought that he committed the murders just by willing it and I let him think that he did. Win, win for everyone!"

It was Marcus' time to talk now. "I appreciate your confession Mr. Abrams. I suspected that you had something to do with this the minute I met you. The very first thing out of your mouth was a lie. You told me that you read all the books in your office. A small lie, nevertheless, a lie. You knew that we were from the homicide division and didn't even ask who had been killed. We looked into your background. You have a Master's Degree in Psychology. You're an expert at analyzing personalities and influencing their behavior. Born with a silver spoon in your mouth. You inherited your business from daddy. He was a criminal and a master manipulator and you turned out to be just like him. I'm sure he would be very proud. And yes, we knew that you visited Sebastian in prison. They keep logs, you know? You were his only visitor for eleven years. The two of you had to be cooking up something!"

"Sebastian doesn't have a dime to his name. You've been financing him ever since he was released. The deed to this cabin where he lived is in your name. You even financed his condo in Southwest. Always follow the money! I knew you weren't doing it out of the kindness of your heart. That would require you to actually have a heart."

"I figured that the two of you committed the murders together, that's why your home is being searched as we speak. I'm sure we'll find something we can use to seal your fate. And thanks for letting me know that you killed them all by yourself. Maybe Sebastian won't have to pay for someone else's crime this time" said Marcus. "That's why I'm here detective. He already paid for his friends crimes and shouldn't have to pay for mine. That wouldn't be fair. I want all the credit for this. Would Picasso want Rembrandt to have the credit for his masterpiece?"

Samuel stood up "I feel a lot better now that I've unburdened myself with these unpleasantries. This couldn't have worked out any better. You know my role in this but no one else will. I can't let you live now, detective. It wouldn't be the prudent thing to do." Marcus stood up "just to let you know Sammy, that clock on the wall (points to it) has a camera in it. There's another camera behind the lamp over there. Oh, and it has sound too. Everyone will know, and if you kill me, you'll get the death penalty for it."

Samuel laughed "what's one more murder on my resume. Got nothing to lose now" as he fires off two shots striking Marcus in the chest. Marcus falls to the ground disorientated and scrambles to pull out his gun. The sound from the gun shot was deafening and left Marcus' ears ringing loudly, not to mention the pain in his chest. It felt as if someone had struck him with a sledge hammer. Samuel shoots him again while he's on the floor trying to scoot away. That bullet strikes him in the thigh, rupturing a major artery. Just then, Logan burst through the back door and tackles Samuel, knocking the gun from his hand. Samuel and Logan quickly rise and face off against each other.

Logan throws a punch at Samuel's head with his right hand. Samuel evades the punch and spins to his left, grabbing Logan's arm and flipping him over his shoulder. Logan hits the floor with a loud thud, knocking the wind out of him. Dazed but not defeated, Logan executes a leg sweep, sending Samuel on his back and to the floor. Samuel does a backwards roll and immediately bounces to his feet with a crazed look. Logan looked into his eyes and for the first time in his career, experienced true fear. Here stood someone that he couldn't intimidate or physically beat.

Before he could rise, the sound of Marcus' gun rings loud. Marcus fires one shot that strikes Samuel in the forehead. Samuel froze for a quick second and his eyes transformed from an evil glare to a lifeless stare as he fell backwards to the floor. As he hit the floor, you could hear the air leave his body as a blast of dust emerged outward from his carcass. Marcus' vision started to blur as his hand went numb and his gun fell to the floor. He slowly laid back and stared at the ceiling as his consciousness began to fade.

Logan quickly pulled out his radio and yelled into it "Officer down, officer down. I need the board (medical board/ambulance) here ASAP! Then he rushed to

Marcus' side "hang on man, help is on the way." He instinctively took off his shirt and used it to tie a tourniquet around Marcus' thigh. Detective Alverez and Sergeant Powell burst through the front door. Sergeant Powell saw how much blood Marcus had lost from his thigh wound and made a command decision "fuck it, we're not waiting for the board, let's put him in your car and take him to the nearest hospital ourselves." They all picked him up and put him in the back of Logan's vehicle, cut on the lights and siren and drove to the hospital like bats outta hell! They radioed the dispatcher, who in turn called the hospital and advised them of their pending arrival.

Once on scene, Logan slammed on the brakes and the tires squealed as the vehicle slid to a stop in front of the emergency room at Charles Regional Medical Center. The ER staff was on standby and quickly pulled Marcus out of the back seat and onto a stretcher. As they rushed him down the hall, Marcus' vision began to dim. He stared up at the ceiling as each fluorescent light fixture raced by. The ER doctors and nurses were talking a mile a minute as they evaluated and treated Marcus. To some it might have looked and sounded chaotic, but in reality it was a symphony of medical science and exactly what he needed.

"BP 82 over palp and falling", "tachypnea at 30." "Take his vest off", "we have diminished breath sounds on the right side, think we're looking at a pneumothorax." "Get me a chest film, AP and lateral." Massive bleeding from his left thigh, the bullet must have hit the femoral artery." "Clamp it and let's hurry up and get him to surgery. He's going into shock, time is not on his side, Go, Go, Go."

Marcus could hear what they were saying in the background but felt his consciousness slipping away. Periods of his life flashed through his mind like a picture show on a giant screen. Marcus clinched his fists and sighed in an attempt to hold onto life. He wasn't ready to die, but how many people really are? Everything seemed to slow down to a standstill. Marcus wondered about his boys. Had he left a good enough example for them? What kind of men would they be as a result of what they saw in him? Would they have to pay for mistakes that he had made in his life?

He started reciting the Lords' Prayer in his mind? Our Father who art in heaven... The last thing that he heard was Logan saying "hold on man, hold on." Then he saw his father smiling, reaching out to him as he nodded in approval before he lost consciousness.

Chapter Twenty
My Brother's Keeper

Marcus came out of surgery in grave condition. The doctors decided to put him in a medically induced coma to help his body heal. They put in a chest tube to heal his lung and repaired the artery in his leg. The surgeon went on to say that, hopefully there would be no permanent damage to the leg. He lost a massive amount of blood but narrowly survived.

After three days he was upgraded to serious condition and they decided to take him out of the coma. As he slowly awoke, Gina and Logan could hear him moan. Everything was fuzzy at first, but his vision slowly began to clear. "Hey babe" he said to Gina. "What happened, where am I" he asked? "You're in the hospital baby, you're gonna be alright" as her tears of happiness began to flow. "No hey baby for me" Logan joked. "Who are you" Marcus asked. Gina and Logan didn't know what to say. Amnesia, maybe? "Just kidding, how could I forget this knuckle head" he said with a painful smile. "Whew, don't scare me like that. I don't know if I can train you all over again" Logan joked.

Marcus spent two weeks in the hospital before he was released to go home. They were able to save his leg and he went through intensive therapy for months before he was able to walk again. In time, he would recover one hundred percent. He wasn't ready to go back to work yet, but Gina took him down to the office to see the squad. As they entered the door, they all cheered for him. "I'm so glad to see you Marcus" said Detective Alverez as she gave him a hug. "You gotta come back soon; this guy (pointing to Logan) is driving me crazy with his singing in the car. And he makes up his own words too." Marcus smiled "not to mention that he's tone deaf." "I ain't deaf" joked Logan.

"Marcus, good to see you brother" said Detective Callahan. "Logan thinks he's in charge with you gone. In your absence, I have realized that he's impervious to rational thinking." "Stop lying, I ain't impotent" responded Logan. Marcus just looked at him and shook his head.

Sergeant Powell stepped up "good to see you Marcus. That was some great police work. We miss you around here but don't hurry back. Get your rest and remember that a wet bird never flies at night." Everyone in the room laughed. As usual, they didn't know what the hell that meant.

Lieutenant O'Malley stepped in "Hey Marcus. Glad you're feeling better. I've got a couple of cases waiting for you when you get back" he joked.

Marcus thanked everyone for their good wishes and support over the last few months. "I'm a little tired now, so I'm gonna go home and enjoy the rest of my time off. I appreciate you guys." Gina looked at Logan and asked "are you still taking him to therapy for me tomorrow?" "Of course Sis" said Logan. "Can you be on time, this time" she asked? Logan scoffed "Of course. You know what they say "the early bird gets to make his nest first." Marcus shook his head "nobody says that." "Yes they do, I hear it all the time" responded Logan. "No they don't" said Marcus. "Yes the do" said Logan. "Oh my God" said Gina. "Are you two married" she joked. They both answered simultaneously "yep, and he's the girl" as they pointed to each other.

   The fact that Marcus was wearing his vest, the first aide rendered by Logan and the decision to transport him to the nearest hospital themselves saved Marcus' life. He needed a blood transfusion and of all people, Logan happened to be the same blood type and donated his blood. A detail that Logan will never let Marcus forget. It was painfully clear that they were all accountable to each other. No one in the squad was perfect. They all had their own set of issues but when they came together as one, they were the perfect squad. Am I my brother's keeper? Yes! Our survival depends on it!

   What we do or don't do as parents, not just fathers but mothers too, can affect our children for decades to come. It can establish generational patterns. Our living example weighs heavily on our children's lives and unconsciously influences their very fiber. If their observations of their parents influence them negatively, they just may have to pay for The Sins of the Father!

www.adwhite.net

Also by A.D. White:

A Killing In D.C., The Chronicles Of Detective Marcus Rose (Volume One)

The Root Of All Evil, The Chronicles of Detective Marcus Rose (Volume Two)

Your feedback is greatly appreciated. Please leave a comment on Amazon.com or at my website, www.adwhite.net

Editors:
Dolores W. Allen
Rosalind N. Moss
Josephine Battle (Mayesville Group Business Consultants)

Cover Illustration by D.J. Jackson, HF Productions